THE CONGRESS OF
ROUGH WRITERS

FLASH FICTION ANTHOLOGY VOL. 1

Michelle,
You are a writer!
Own your stories,
even the ones you
collect.
Love
Charli

Published by Carrot Ranch Literary Community.
Series Editor, Charli Mills
Editor, Sarah Brentyn
ISBN: 978-1-54391-795-6 (print)
ISBN: 978-1-54391-796-3 (ebook)

We dedicate this anthology to the literary community at Carrot Ranch: The Rough Writers, the Friends who write with us, the Readers, and the unknown Lurkers who think they might try to write a flash one day (do it!). May we continue to inspire one another like pilgrims on a journey. First we were strangers, and then we wrote together.

TABLE OF CONTENTS

FOREWORD

By Charli Mills, Series Editor

Legend of Carrot Ranch (in 99 Words)

A buckaroo called Charli once decided between saddle and pen. She chased an ink trail across the Rockies to the city-slicker lights of the Midwest, branding businesses with stories.

That's where she discovered carrots — the power symbol for food justice. The buckaroo thought, literary justice is words for people.

One day, the ink trail returned west, toward tales and sunsets. Charli found a place to settle her pen and she called it Carrot Ranch. Other word wranglers joined the movement, writing weekly flash fiction — 99 words, no more, no less.

That's the legend, and Charli is sticking to it.

Carrot Ranch began the day I decided to go after the literary prize of my dreams and win the equivalent of a rodeo buckle in publishing: my first novel. Like many writers, I enabled this dream through years of writing journals and incomplete drafts, joining a writers group, and attending annual workshops. I had established my career as a business writer and freelancer focused on the faces and places of organic and local food systems. Food justice reoccurred as a theme within the community food movement. It had to do with making wholesome food accessible to everyone, especially the most vulnerable and marginalized populations.

This got me to thinking about the accessibility of literary art. How do we reach others outside of traditional academic circles to play with words and improve our craft? The community food movement showed me that even a small group of focused individuals could create tremendous synergy. My understanding of community relationships encouraged me to create a welcoming platform for word play where literary writers could connect. Carrot Ranch exists in the virtual world, but it's a solid community.

Carrot Ranch has no minimum requirements to respond to its weekly flash fiction challenges, nor does it offer critique. The idea is to create safe space that allows for exploration, connection, and education. Writers who want to play or authors who take a break for fun are welcome among the more serious short story crafters. No one is judging, comparing, or competing. Each writer can study craft or simply play.

Literary artists continue to hone their craft throughout their lives, but don't often allow time to play with craft or ideas. The weekly flash fiction challenges offer constraints within the invitation to play with words. One is meant to be the flint that sparks an idea. That's the prompt. It's open to interpretation, and writers are encouraged to go where it leads, even if it's dark, humorous, or seemingly unrelated. The second constraint limits each response to 99 words, no more, no less. It's meant to act as a problem the mind has to solve. Some writers approach the constraint by writing freely and whittling words, whereas others execute an idea within the framework. Some even volunteer an additional constraint of poetic form.

Raw literature, those first works we create as literary artists, can result from word play. Often we refer to first drafts as tainted, recognizing the work of revision yet to come. But when we call our early works "dirty first drafts," we diminish the value of our creative process. Playing with flash fiction becomes a way to value the creative process and honor the work necessary to polish 99 words into a literary gem. When writers feel secure in sharing raw drafts among polished forms, we all get to observe both creativity and craft in action. I've watched regular writers at Carrot Ranch play with twists (which work well in short form and also become a linchpin to ending book chapters). I've marveled at others who employ true stories as a way to use the challenge to explore their memoir work.

The regular writers at Carrot Ranch became The Congress of Rough Writers, a name derived from Buffalo Bill Cody's international Wild West show. As lead buckaroo for the literary community, I give the space a western flavor, but that doesn't mean we all write historical fiction. On the contrary, what makes the literary community dynamic is the diversity of writers who gather. We write across all genres, including specific fictions, memoir, poetry, education material, and science journalism. It fits the idea of Buffalo Bill's troupe of daring feats because he also gathered a Congress of Rough Riders, claiming in an 1889 Annual that "the whole ensemble is totally dissimilar from anything the ingenuity of man has heretofore conceived or devised." Buffalo Bill's show differed from others because he presented an amalgamation of those who were true to their own style of riding.

As a literary community, Carrot Ranch allows writers the freedom to write as they are and what they please (provided, of course, it's 99 words, no more, no less). I can imagine the nomads, tribesmen, and frontiersmen who rode for Buffalo Bill, learning from one another in moments of appreciation and shared skill. I've learned about genres outside my own, and a fair number of memoirists who thought they would never write fiction discovered they liked it. These same memoirists also taught the rest of us a hybrid of creative writing known as BOTS, which is fiction based on a true story.

Each week, I compile the gathered responses to create a unique literary performance from the prompt-based word play. Readers find much to consider among the comparisons, contrasts, perspectives, and structures conveyed. I say, with regularity, the compilation is my favorite part of the flash fiction challenges. I never know how the overall tone of stories will emerge. It's become an inside ranch joke — don't give these writers rainbows and unicorns because they'll go deep and dark. (That's a hint not to miss the last chapter from Part 1: Best of Show.)

Another interesting attribute of an online literary community is country of origin. Just like Buffalo Bill's Congress was not all American, neither is the Carrot Ranch Congress. Rough Writers hail from across the globe — the United States, Canada, Australia, the United Kingdom, Poland, and Spain. The friends who join us weekly (new or intermittent writers) are also diverse. The appeal is an authentic community where writers are welcome to craft without critique or expectation. We're as friendly as a western campfire at dinnertime on the long trail to pursue literary art. Each Rough Writer's byline in this anthology denotes country of origin, and we've allowed for an editing process that honors both American and British styles of English. After all, Buffalo Bill would not have expected a nomad to ride the same saddle as a roper in his Wild West show. Diversity is our strength.

When Buffalo Bill sat on his horse and watched the Congress ride, I know how he felt, witnessing each daring feat. I recognize the styles of each Rough Writer, and yet they continue to delight and surprise me. They also inspire me in my own writing. I wanted to put together an anthology of our work that expanded what we do at Carrot Ranch each week. We entertain readers and provoke thoughtful response. An anthology can also be educational. Fellow Rough Writer Sarah Brentyn, a writing teacher, shared a vision for the educational potential of an anthology. As editor, she has guided the development of this book. Her keen insights for structure and literary credibility are invaluable. She worked with all twenty-eight writers to expand the scope of this book beyond the original 99-word stories we developed in 2014.

PART 1: BEST OF SHOW is twelve collections of ten 99-word stories. Each chapter in this part is titled according to the prompt given in the challenge. There is a vast variety in the responses, yet each individual flash fiction completes the whole. The stories are arranged in a creative way to make a greater statement. Sometimes the connections are overt, sometimes the stories contrast, and other times one story holds an idea expanded in the next. Book clubs can use this collection to discuss how the prompts were managed. Writers and non-writers can try their hand at penning a 99-word response to each prompt.

CHAPTER 1

Flash Fiction Challenge: In 99 words (no more, no less) write a story that demonstrates compassion.

Embracing the Individual by Geoff Le Pard (UK)

The girl laid flowers on the mossy grave. 'What was grandpa like, Dad?'

Her father said, 'He was a mixture of things, love. Kind, caring...'

'At school they say he was gay.'

'Yes. He was. After he divorced grandma he realised...'

'And they say he had a weird religion.'

Her father forced a small smile. 'A Buddhist. Not many in Liverpool.'

'And he lived with a black man.'

Her father knelt down. 'Those things are just dull wrapping paper. You have to rip that off to find the gift inside. Everyone is different but everyone is still a gift.'

Understanding by Norah Colvin (AU)

In the *smart* outfit carefully selected by the charity shop attendant, Marnie was surprised how well the confident exterior masked the whirlpool of fear, anxiety, and insecurity.

Without looking up, the receptionist handed Marnie a number and waved her to the waiting area.

"9." Her heart sank. "That many?"

Avoiding contact and *contamination*, she squeezed into the only available space: between a boy slouching awkwardly and a girl picking her fingernails.

The girl started crying. Marnie stiffened, but glanced sideways. The girl cried into her sleeve.

Marnie breathed, proffered her unopened purse packet of just-in-case tissues, and smiled, "Here."

Compassion by Irene Waters (AU)

So beautiful. No external mark hinted at the catastrophic injuries she had sustained in the crash. She was my patient, and I would give her the last dignities of life despite the tubes which gave her breath and drained her fluids.

"I'll get security. The boyfriend's getting angry. I've told him it's relatives only. Some people." My colleague went off, her huff travelling with her.

Some people indeed, I thought. I couldn't leave my charge. I called over another colleague, who did my bidding.

The boyfriend stood behind the closed curtain with me. Tears streamed from four eyes. We hugged.

Compassion for the Relationship by Anne Goodwin (UK)

We never reserved *I love you* for Valentine's and anniversaries, so why should it matter that, this year, you forgot? Yet I contemplate arsenic-on-toast for your breakfast; you couldn't even bring me a cup of tea in bed.

Once you're cleaned, fed, and dressed, we wait for the sitter. The hairdresser's booked and the theatre, a restaurant reservation for one.

This evening, when I'm calm again, we'll look through the photographs. "Who's that handsome man with the carnation buttonhole?" I'll say. I won't mind if you can't tell me; my memories of our marriage are strong enough for two.

Her Worth by Charli Mills (US)

The old mare hung her head low, lips quivering above grass-forsaken dirt, ribs protruding beneath a swayed back. She was broken.

"How much you want for her," asked the Fed Ex driver.

A lean cowboy scrawled his signature for his box. "That nag?"

"That our wine?" A beautiful woman stepped out onto the deck.

The cowboy winked at the Fed Ex man. "There's a beauty worth buying."

"Can't afford that one. How much for the horse?"

He knew his boss would ask how a starving mare got into the back of his van, but already her ears had perked.

A Plate of Food by Ruchira Khanna (US)

Sarita opened the door to her maid, who had brought her kid to work.

"He is my son, Jay," introduced the maid with pride.

"Friends?" Sarita's son, Hari, extended his hands towards him.

"Sure," nodded Jay and they walked towards the toys.

While playing, Sarita brought a plate of food for her son.

Jay pretended to play while Hari was being fed. Just then, a morsel came towards him.

He looked up to see Hari's hand holding a snack.

With moist eyes, he took the grub and soon both the boys were munching and giggling away.

Compassionate Neighbours by Susan Zutautas (CA)

Easter was approaching and there was barely enough food to feed the family of six let alone get the children any chocolate eggs or bunnies.

'Stop worrying Agnes, surely some work will turn up soon', said Roy.

Normally he was right but Agnes felt deep in her heart that this year there'd be no ham on their table for dinner.

It was Good Friday and Agnes heard a knock at the door. No one was there but there was a fairly large box sitting on the porch. It was filled with food, chocolate, and a ham.

Agnes' heart melted.

Invisible by Sarah Brentyn (US)

"We're late!" Jeremy snatched his coat from the closet. "Mum!"

"I know! Stop...stop yelling. We'll be right there."

"Mum, seriously! Coach will bench me!"

The clicking of cleats on tile echoed down the hallway. Jeremy's face tightened with each step. He swung into the kitchen. "If I have to sit this game out I'll..."

His mother sat on the floor stroking his little brother's hair as he reached out again and again, touching the edge of the countertop. She didn't look up. "We'll be right there."

"No, it's good." Jeremy crouched down. "We'll go when you're ready, okay buddy?"

No One Should Have It Coming by Amber Prince (US)

"He's a troublemaker."

"He has been in trouble before, but I wouldn't call him a troublemaker."

"Does it matter? It wasn't that big of a deal."

"It does matter, it's a big deal, he came to you for help, and you ignored him."

"I heard what he had to say, but how was I to know that the other kid was going to actually do something? That one is a good student."

"And now?"

"What do you want me to say? That I'm sorry? Fine, but the boy had it coming."

"You're wrong. No one should have it coming."

Coffee Break by Larry LaForge (US)

Robert scooted from his early morning sociology class to the coffee shop downtown.

Turning onto Main, he spotted someone sitting on the corner holding a crude cardboard sign: A FRIEND IN NEED. He watched as many passersby nodded with sympathy but generally avoided eye contact. Some folks tossed coins into the box without missing a step as they continued on.

Robert checked his pocket for cash, entered the cafe, and ordered two large coffees to go.

"Cream and sugar?" Robert asked as he plopped down next to the vagrant.

They talked for two hours about sports, weather and politics.

CHAPTER 2

*Flash Fiction Challenge: In 99 words (no more, no less) write
a story using two objects, people, or ideas that don't go together.*

—————•◆•————

Questions and Cigarettes by Anne Goodwin (UK)

"Does your home have more rooms than people?"

Matty stared as if I were the crazy one.

I ticked the "no" box and moved on. "Can you make a meal any time
you choose?"

Matty frowned. "May I see?"

I passed the questionnaire across. How to explain our duty, not only to ensure
a better quality of life in the community, but to prove it?

Matty dragged on her cigarette. She raised a corner of the printed sheet to
meet the glowing tip.

I would've scored that as another "no", had she not reduced the questionnaire
to black powder.

Perfect Happiness by Georgia Bell (US)

She rubbed a thumb over her chapped knuckle, her manicured hands thaw-
ing from the cold. The woman who sat across the aisle from her smiled warmly and
nodded, before returning to her crossword. Ellie stared at her, noting the wisps of
hair straggling from her bun, the scuff marks on her boots, the frayed cotton bag

tucked beside her full of knitting needles and yarn. Her stomach twisted with an envy she could barely contain. How could this disheveled woman be so content, so at peace, when Ellie had worked so hard to be perfect and was so miserable?

This Christmas? by Ruchira Khanna (US)

I was taking a walk around my neighborhood when suddenly there was a loud thunder followed by torrential downpour. That made me duck under the roof of a home. I started hearing some familiar, but loud voices coming from the four walls.

Could not resist, I walked around the home, to be able to recognize those sounds that seemed to have quite a conversation. As I glanced through the window; I jumped in horror.

Took physically broad steps towards my home; sure that a catastrophe is about to strike since Santa and the Grinch are under the same roof.

Halloween by Pete Fanning (US)

Dustin's phone buzzed just as he snuck underneath the yellow light.

"Will you pick up some apples?"

"Apples?"

"Yeah, the kids want apples."

"On Halloween?"

"Yep."

"Okay, got it."

Inside, Dustin remembered that he wanted to repaint the window sills. After a quick detour he found an open register.

"You're like, serious?" the young cashier said. The sun angled into the store.

"I'm like, what?" Dustin asked. The woman behind him snickered.

"You should call the cops."

Dustin turned to face the woman just as the girl held up his purchase like evidence. "Razor blades and apples, on Halloween?"

Sweet and Sour Smoke by Geoff Le Pard (UK)

Mary jumped.

'Mum, are you smoking?'

Mary dropped the cigarette, grinding it out. 'Sorry, love.'

'I thought you'd given up?'

'I had. I…'

'Wait there.'

Mary marvelled at how like Mary's mother Penny sounded. She had had a way of tightening her mouth, emphasising each syllable; Penny was the same. Mary smiled. It was oddly comforting, having someone else take charge.

Penny held a little bottle. 'I'm putting this on the cigarettes. Like you did to stop me chewing my nails.'

Later when Mary lit up, she felt real joy; such a sour taste had never tasted so sweet.

Water and Electricity by Sherri Matthews (UK)

Mavis's eyes flew open as the front door slammed.

"Goddamit, Frank, what the hell time do you call this? You were supposed to be home two hours ago."

Frank stumbled into the bathroom, grinning drunkenly from ear to ear.

"Sorry honey…"

"Yeah right. Hand me that towel, you useless drunk." Mavis glowered as she attempted to pull herself up to standing.

Frank swivelled to reach for the towel and lost his balance, accidentally swiping the hair dryer off its shelf.

The last thing Mavis heard was the click of the on-switch as the hair dryer flew into the bath.

Guns and Apples by Charli Mills (US)

The sweet smell of rotting apples wafted across the meadow on west-slanting rays of sunshine. It was late afternoon and time to start dinner. Ramona shifted her prone position in tall grass to ease the pain of old arthritic knees. The VA had more paperwork for her to file before they'd pay out widow's benefits. The last can of pinto beans was simmering on the stove back at the house. Something had to give, and soon.

A breaking twig snapped. Dry leaves crumpled. The buck had come to eat apples. She steadied her dead husband's rifle for her provision.

Gun and Bun by Irene Waters (AU)

Janelle felt the men watching. She affected them with her perfect body. And she was pretty if not beautiful, although she had to say it herself. Why didn't they ask her out? She was a girly girl. Even her iPhone was pink.

"A bun please." Her soft, sensual voice floated to the watching men but their eyes had gravitated to her hip. The gun resting in the holster, as cold and hard as the buns she was buying were soft and doughy. She wept, realising the buns were more desired than she.

Confidence and Fear by Larry LaForge (US)

He was the envy of friends and foes alike. Wagner seemed in absolute control at all times — comfortable in his own skin, as they say.

The crowd waited in the Grand Ballroom with great anticipation. His name would be called shortly, and Wagner would accept the nomination.

In a remote bathroom in the hotel's back corridor, Wagner hunched over the toilet. Sweat pouring from his forehead, he heaved almost uncontrollably, making sure his expensive suit was out of harm's way. He had perfected the technique.

Less than thirty minutes later, Wagner wowed the audience with his brilliant acceptance speech.

Unicorn and Coffee by Norah Colvin (AU)

People crammed in, around, and in front of the small sidewalk cafe, reminding her of the fairy-tale pageant that had bypassed her radar. She couldn't move now. Her coffee fix, too hot to sip, had just been served. So, as always, she retreated within.

Cocooned in thoughts flittering across years and experiences, she barely noticed the cacophony of the crowd or passing parade.

The sudden shout of "Unicorn!" penetrated, and it startled her.

She was six again, cowering with her unicorn, avoiding mocking stares.

But this time pitying and unbelieving stares watched the spreading stain of her scalding coffee.

CHAPTER 3

Flash Fiction Challenge: In 99 words (no more, no less) write a story that considers history, near or far.

Ghost Town by Amber Prince (US)

She walked alone down the dirt road, once inundated with horses and maybe carriages even, trying to feel some connection to her past. Had any of her family skipped stones in the stream nearby or stopped for a drink after a hard day of mining?

Her fingers itched to run themselves over the weathered wood of buildings. She passed an old saloon that had once been the livelihood of this town. Eyes closed, she inhaled the clean mountain air and tried to imagine the old ghost town come to life.

What had scared an entire town enough to run?

Rope Swings by Sarah Brentyn (US)

I am Bridget.

They think I am dead.

In a way, I suppose I am. Yet I watch my town dissolve into fits worse than the girls claiming to be afflicted. Salem has become a carnival of fear, hysteria, and retaliation. Panic and pettiness result in neighbors and friends swinging by the neck. I was the first to hang. Still, I watch. I see townsfolk accuse and kill.

The irony tickles me. I am, indeed, a witch.

The devil they believe in does not exist. Evil does. It resides not in witchcraft but in the actions of ordinary people.

Washing Day by Norah Colvin (AU)

Her freckled, calloused hands were red and chaffed as they gripped the wooden stick and stirred Monday's sheets in the large copper pot heating over burning blocks of wood.

The children played in the dirt nearby, scratching like chickens, hopeful of an interesting find.

The dirt embedded under her torn and splitting fingernails began to ease away in the warm sudsy water as she heaved the sodden sheets and plopped them onto the wooden mangles.

The children fought to turn the handle, smearing dirty handprints on the sheets.

She sighed and hung them over the line. One chore done.

True Calling by Sherri Matthews (UK)

Madeline Dorothy was stubborn and she knew what she wanted to do with her life. Looking after her mother wasn't it.

Brought up as a Baptist minister's daughter, the middle child with two brothers during the tail end of Edwardian Britain, there was every expectation that she would forgo a career and stay at home.

The Roaring Twenties charged in and when Madeline announced that she wanted to pursue a nursing career in London, it did not go down well. She ran away and fulfilled her ambition of nursing sick children.

It was years before Madeline's mother forgave her.

The Refuge by Lisa Reiter (UK)

She should try harder; then it might not have been necessary. There must be something wrong with her. Was she so inadequate she didn't know how to keep her man happy? Ugo Cerletti was responsible for the latest insult to treat her *marriage problems.*

Now her man was out, the decision already made and no going back. She gathered the children and ran — afraid he would catch her first.

She borrowed money from neighbours for the bus and finally she was at Belmont Terrace being enveloped by Erin in hope and hugs.

"Come in Jenny. You're safe with us."

Garden Rhododendrons by Anne Goodwin (UK)

My sister dived into the shrubbery. "She'll never look for us here."

I bit my lip. "But it's cheating."

Across the park, Mum was calling: "Coming, ready or not!"

She wasn't like the other mothers, too busy to chat or play. Mum bubbled with stories of her carefree childhood at the big house, of games of hide and seek with handsome stable boys.

"Come on!" My sister grabbed my hand from between the leaves, a purple flower crowning her head like a giant bow. Sick rose to my throat. Mum hated rhododendrons the way I hated geometry and spinach.

Inherent by Pete Fanning (US)

I'm usually outside when it comes. I'll be cutting grass or tinkering with the old car, getting grit in my nails and sweating when I think, *Papa would have laughed at that.*

I use his old tools that I keep in my basement. He had a place for everything, pipe cleaners, nuts and bolts, wrenches, the screwdrivers with the worn wooden handles that still work so well.

He was a great man, my grandfather, and those brief flashes of the past give me a shiver of pride. Because — if just for a second — he's right there by my side.

You Can't Take It with You by Geoff Le Pard (UK)

Mary opened the desk drawer. What a mess. She needed help with Dad's estate.

Underneath some bills she found a postcard: Brighton, postmarked 1984. 'Darling Peter, we have to stop.' Signed 'Angela'.

Mary remembered the strange woman at the funeral, calling herself Angie. 'We need to talk.' Handing her a phone number.

Memories flooded back.

Mum crying. 'Why with Angela?'

Seeing a list of Dad's standing orders. '£100 to Ms A Simmonds each month.'

A trip to town. Bumping into a woman and red-haired boy. Dad embarrassed. Boy's hair like Dad's in those old photos.

What a mess.

My Ancestor, Peter Stille by Paula Moyer (US)

Peter had been a Huguenot (French Protestant) all his life. His parents had converted before he was born. All had been well. Now Louis XIV decreed that Huguenots had three choices: become Catholic, leave, or be killed.

He hadn't saved enough money for his fare for the ship to England, but time was running out. He had just enough to bribe a crew member. The night before embarking, he slid into the cargo hold as a stowaway.

Next morning, choppy waters. He threw up in a corner. Finally, the ship docked. He waited for darkness. Slid out into freedom.

Amelia by Irene Waters (AU)

Amelia left the two women who stared after her.

"Amelia's in the family way again."

"Every time that ne'er-do-well husband comes home she has another bairn."

"Lucky his ship don't come in too oft. Threes enough on yer own..."

***

One hundred and ten years later Amelia's great-grandchildren scoured through Ancestry.com. Little was known of their great-grandfather apart from his birth date in Boston, Massachusetts. The last time the family saw him was 1904.

"I've found something." We poured over the 1910 marriage certificate — to another woman. Not only new aunts, uncles, and cousins but a skeleton in the closet. Great-Grand Dad was a bigamist.

CHAPTER 4

Flash Fiction Challenge: In 99 words (no more, no less) write a photo bomb (serious scene interrupted by something absurd or unexpected).

———◆•◆•◆———

Busted by Larry LaForge (UK)

A local news photographer positioned himself to get a great shot. The legendary groundhog would emerge any second.

Would actions of the simple groundhog signal more winter weather or the advent of spring?

The photographer took a picture just as the cage opened and the famous marmot appeared.

As the crowd cheered, the photographer checked the pic on his camera's screen. He noticed something strange in the bottom right corner. He zoomed in, squinting his eyes.

Whattha?

He zoomed in further and was shocked at what he saw hidden in groundhog's cage:

Mini weather satellite and meteorological communications receiver.

→←

A Hike to Remember by Ruchira Khanna (US)

Laura and her family went on a hike in the woods. The surroundings were serene except for a bunch of squirrels who would go hither and thither. That would make them pause in their steps by giving these little creatures the way.

Seeing them nibble cutely on their food, she showed interest in being clicked with one of them.

Her son brought her and the little creature into one frame and was about to click when his eyes widened, and he screamed in horror.

Curious Laura turned around and, to her dismay, she saw a bear in the background.

An Order of Valor to Go... by Pete Fanning (US)

We'd just come out of the bathroom, ready to hit the road. I had my phone recording — because Chris had never been in Virginia — when the two girls in pajamas entered. There was some arguing, something about breakfast hours having passed. Then the heavier one tossed the chair and it clanged against the window.

Grandma didn't even flinch. She looked the girls over calmly and said, "Someone loves you." The heavyset one froze mid-heave. Glaring, tears bloomed from her worried eyes. Then she slammed the chair down and ran right out of the store.

I hoped Grandma was right.

My Boyfriend by Georgia Bell (UK)

He hunched over on the cold bench, head sagging and elbows heavy on his thighs. "I love you, I do. I just feel like we're so disconnected."

Wrapping her arms around her waist, she shivered, feeling the wind bite at the skin of her cheeks, raw with tears.

A shadow fell over them, blocking the sun, and she looked up to see a man dressed in tight black clothes, his face white, beret askew. Eyes wide, the man pantomimed climbing a ladder and being trapped in a prison.

"Fuck off, mime," they said in unison and smiled, hands reaching.

Rabbit Ears by Sherri Matthews (UK)

Carrie was losing patience as fast as her head pounded. Grabbing Mikey's hand while simultaneously jostling his baby sister out of her stroller, she warned him to stay by her side.

"I'm bored…!" Mikey protested.

"Stay here!" hissed Carrie, "Look, we're up next…!"

"Well, hi there, kids! All ready for your photo?" beamed the cameraman.

An hour later, Carrie sighed as she selected the best of the shoot: the baby smiled as red, sticky juice dribbled off her chin and Mikey grimaced while making rabbit ears behind his sister's head.

It would have to do — the perfect Christmas photo.

The New Cameraman by Charli Mills (US)

"Is my collar straight, Bob?" Cynthia of the Morning Show stared coolly at the set manager. Bob grimaced and gave her a thumb's up.

"Bob, is that light skewed?"

Bob climbed the catwalk and gave Cynthia thumbs up.

"Good morning, Cynthia! I love your show. I'm…"

Cynthia cut off gushing with a guillotine stare. Bob looked at the new cameraman and shook his head, no. Cynthia smiled like a coyote with a dead rabbit. "No talking to me on set."

Cameras rolled and the new man grinned. He could see the spinach in her perfect teeth. But no talking.

Taking the Piss by Geoff Le Pard (UK)

'Closer, Uncle Rupert! You too, Mum.' Penny waved for Mary to move nearer.

Reluctantly Mary and her half-brother stood side by side.

While Penny adjusted her camera, he whispered, 'How's the mother hunt going?'

Mary detected a smirk in his voice.

'You worked out father's secret yet?'

Mary began to speak when she noticed some spilled tea had left an embarrassing stain by his fly.

She surprised him by taking his arm. 'Try now, Penny.'

She hoped the angle worked. In any case, she intended to ensure he pissed himself for real by the time she finished her research.

Assassin by Sarah Brentyn (US)

He couldn't do it.

For some reason, he couldn't kill this one. He leaned in and stared at the eyes. He had never spent any time actually looking before. Sitting back on his heels, he felt the weight of the weapon in his hand.

He thought about the term "taking a life." What was he taking? Ending a life. That's what he was doing — what he had done countless times before. He would stop a heart. He would prevent any more air entering lungs. He would crush a body.

"Bloody hell, Carl! Haven't you killed that damn spider yet?"

Offertory Giggle-Bomb by Paula Moyer (US)

That Sunday morning, Jean was thrilled to meet Sally. Her boyfriend Teddy was excited. His older sister was home for the summer.

Jean was nervous. She and Teddy sat behind Sally and her friends. Sally was gorgeous, with black, curly hair and doll-like features. And she was a college girl. Jean was barely fourteen.

Then came the offertory. When the maple offering basket came down their aisle, it was full of the usual coins, bills, and offering envelopes. On top, inexplicably, lay a tortoise-shell barrette.

Jean saw the barrette and giggled. Thought about it and giggled. She couldn't stop.

Video Bombing by Norah Colvin (AU)

Are you a video bomber?
Ever tried making a video but
the subject won't cooperate,
or turns its back to you,
or perhaps it even disappears *Poof!* It's out of view.
You shoot upside down or to the side,
the focus you can't get right.
You shoot with the camera supposedly off,
then close-up your fingers when on.
You record to capture a photo,
or snap when it's action you want.
If your answer is "Yes" to just one of these
come join the video-bombers club.
First we'll commiserate
And then we'll celebrate
When your video captures "the bomb"!

CHAPTER 5

Flash Fiction Challenge: In 99 words (no more, no less) write story about water.

Blackouts on the Rise by Susan Zutautas

Temperatures expected to rise to 132 today. I know, folks. This has not been a pleasant summer, and with all the water alerts it doesn't make life on the Mojave very comfortable. I do wish I had some relief for you in sight but sadly do not. Please try and use your fans rather than your A/C due to blackouts occurring throughout the west.

Fines will be increased to 2500.00 for anyone caught wasting water. This includes gardens, lawns, cars, and pools, until further notice.

Sighing deeply, I wound up my crank radio, yearning to hear some good news.

Water Flash by Anne Goodwin (UK)

We pulled up alongside a wooden shack with a blistered Coca-Cola sign above the entrance. The driver had barely stepped inside the ramshackle shop when they came, swarming round the windows of the SUV with their cupped hands and pleading faces.

It was sweltering inside without the aircon. When the driver returned bearing gallon bottles of water, we gave him a round of applause.

Leaving the village, we pointed our cameras at the shallow river where women scrubbed rainbow-coloured clothes and children splashed in the shallows. Where, in rusting cans and old oil drums, girls harvested the household's water.

Cruel Summer by Pete Fanning (US)

Phillip squinted at the sparkling pool, rippling with playful screams and splashes and colorful pool toys from one end to the other. He sat down next to his mom on a lounge chair, already drenched in sweat as the sun burned through his shirt.

"Hey, Phillip, you getting in?" Owen asked from the edge. Phillip watched the water dripping off his skinny arms.

"Maybe later."

He'd been so fearless before and felt the stares clinging to him like his shirt on his hips. Today he would wait until dark, when he'd plunge into the still water shirtless and alone.

The Cleansing by Geoff Le Pard (UK)

Mary shuddered. His hands were sticky with sweat; it felt like he'd wiped himself dry on her.

'It's brilliant to meet you at last. It's been far too long.'

Rupert Reeves. Her half-brother, though when she looked at him her mind screamed, 'Dad's bastard'.

Even his voice seemed to ooze over her, coating her in damp guilt. 'Why did our parents never introduce us?'

She tried a smile. 'It was difficult.'

'Your mother, yes? She couldn't forgive, could she?'

Later Mary stood under the shower and scrubbed herself raw. Why did he assume anyone would forgive her father's affair?

Water Flash by Georgia Bell (CA)

The glass felt heavy in her hands, a welcome weight in contrast to her racing thoughts. Inhaling, she felt her heartbeat slow. Amber and toffee and a dash of pepper invaded her senses with nostalgia. Every breath reminding her of his warm, rich voice, his large hands showing her how to tie her shoes and catch tadpoles. Hands that had tucked her in each night, with a kiss and prayer to a god he didn't believe in. "No water," he'd said. "If you want to experience something, don't dilute it. Dive in." She drank the scotch in his memory.

Tree of Life by Lisa Reiter (UK)

It was dry and dusty and the waterhole had turned to mud. Fish slopped pathetically, where once he drank and played. With nothing to stay for, his mother urged him away, although the horizon only shimmered dangerously with mirage. She'd been calling the gods of thunder but he was afraid of them. And he had never been thirsty.

She marched with certainty towards scrubland on the horizon. After many hours she trumpeted delight, sighting an ancient baobab.

Pulling bark from the tree, she offered him its miraculous water. He would remember where to come next time the rains failed.

Greatest of the Great Lakes by Paula Moyer (US)

Jean never took the "Express Highway" up the North Shore of Lake Superior. It was always the scenic route. Even then, "scenic" really took off north of Two Harbors.

She hungered to memorize the twists and turns of Highway 61. Turn, turn, turn. Glimpse, glimpse, glimpse through trees. Then: big hilltop vista, carpet laced with glittering blue diamonds. She could hear a kettle drum with each viewing.

Somewhere north of Gooseberry Falls, she would enact her ritual. Walk to shore, place towel on rock. Remove shoes. Wade in up to the knees. Cherished, cold shock. Liquid ice, beloved lake.

Tolo Lake Graveyard by Charli Mills (US)

One Saturday morning local volunteers gathered around the small mud flat littered with dead branches. The local Chamber had donated coffee.

"Listen up," called out the state biologist. "We've drained water from Tolo and with your help we'll begin mucking out the bottom to improve fishing."

"Damn snags," said a Grangeville farmer, swishing the last of his coffee. "I'm gonna find those Castmasters." He walked over to the largest branch, wiped away black mud, recognized a bone. All the branches were bone.

Tolo Lake, a small water artesian in the middle of farmland, was a mass graveyard of mammoths.

A Village No More by Sherri Matthews (UK)

Dark, orange sky urged Mary to quicken her step as she walked by the side of the lake. At last, she found the clearing.

Stopping to check her watch, nothing but the sound of the water gently lapping against the lakeshore broke the silence.

Then it happened: the lake turned still as a millpond. Mary heard the first chime of the bells before she high-tailed it out of there. The old village had been purposely flooded to make the reservoir and locals spoke of hearing church bells on certain summer nights.

She hadn't believed them but she did now.

A Stormy Dance by Amber Prince (US)

The waltz of the storm raced along the curvy paths, cutting a new trail with a torrential wet force. It looked as though a thick, gray blanket fell from the sky, covering the mountains from sight. Lightning danced to and fro from the clouds, wreaking havoc wherever its electrified slashes touched. The musical tune, played by the thunder, boomed across the peaks as it kept the beat.

It was coming my way. There was nowhere to go, so I watched. Waited. Thirsty. Panic and hunger battled inside me for I would live or die.

Because a plant can't run.

CHAPTER 6

Flash Fiction Challenge: In 99 words (no more, no less) write a story that features an angel.

———————◆●◆●◆———————

Angelic Protection by Paula Moyer (US)

Two hours behind schedule. Jean stewed about it all day. Her husband had puttered. The long drive up I-35, the last leg of their vacation, waited for them.

Just into Minnesota, the flashing lights of a dozen patrol cars pulled her out of her stew. She stared at the accident scene, car-become-accordion. No ambulance — no survivors?

Jean switched her gaze back to the interstate. Oh, no — two men on the road? Oh. Yes. Oblivious. Then she blinked. Shadows.

The next morning, she googled and found it: wrong-way head-on crash. Right there.

Two hours before.

Not shadows.

Not men.

Angels.

➤←

Archangel by Larry LaForge (US)

The surly government agent meant business. "You can't perform angelic acts without a license, ma'am."

"Since when?" the serene woman with heavenly blue eyes asked.

"Look, lady, just pay the fee. The government doesn't care if you're bogus or legit. We just need you to register and pay up."

"But I work for a higher power."

"There's no higher power than the government, ma'am."

After a few moments, the angel decided to end the standoff. She could have made the agent disappear, but instead removed herself gracefully, evaporating before his eyes.

"You still have to register," the agent yelled.

I Quit by Sarah Brentyn (US)

She hadn't planned to show herself.

His lungs were filling with water — she panicked, materializing and assuring him she would always protect him.

It was a mistake. He filled the next year with stupid stunts.

"Check it out," he shouted, jumping off the bridge. "I've got a guardian angel! I can't die!"

His angel appeared, much clearer than she had the first time.

"You're looking haggard," he chuckled and rubbed the back of his head. His hand was wet. Glaring at her, he brought his fingers to his face. Blood. "What the hell?"

"I'm sorry." She smiled. "Good luck."

Lips of an Angel by Georgia Bell (US)

"You're my angel," he said, brushing the hair back from her eyes.

Her face hidden, she nodded, but her heart dropped and disappointment loomed.

It always ended the same way.

Months later, she jammed her clothes into the suitcase, scanning the apartment for the last of her belongings. Her eyes rested on the photograph, framed carefully.

His wild hair now tamed. His piercings gone. His eyes, clear and loving as they gazed at her.

She walked out and slammed the door behind her.

She was looking for the one who wouldn't change to please her.

She liked them bad.

Angel Flash Fiction by Anne Goodwin (UK)

The Angel of Death raged through our people, anointing us with yellow stars. Some perished in gas ovens, others by disease and starvation; some survived through happenstance, determination, and guile. Even once the purge was over, we were forced from the debris of our homes. Exiled among strangers, the less we remembered, the more we grew content.

Years passed before they came for our stories, armed with notebooks and pens. What did these well-fed youths know of suffering? What did they care? Yet when they promised compensation, we opened up our hearts. The Avenging Angel had arrived at last.

Gift Exchange by Charli Mills (US)

That first Christmas after Papa died, Mama took a town job, waiting tables. While she was working, Clive and Maggie decorated the spruce next to Papa's grave near their ranch. They hung shining red balls, silver bells, and Papa's favorite collection of glittering musical instruments. The next morning, they took Mama to the tree. A crow flew past with a harp hanging from his beak. Mama began to cry.

Maggie glared at her brother. "Clive, that crow took Papa's favorite ornaments!"

"Children, it's okay. Look what he left." She pointed to the pile of gold coins on Papa's headstone.

Naked Angels by Jeanne Belisle Lombardo (US)

He was dead; he was alive; he was somewhere with a needle in his arm. Only one thing was sure. Her son wouldn't be home for Christmas this year.

She reached for the next small box amidst the flurry of crumpled tissue paper and discarded containers. "Naked Angels" the label read. She smiled. Thought of Tom, who had given the Mexican folk figures to her at successive college Christmas parties.

She picked one up: a male angel in a deep lacquered purple-blue; fierce countenance; wings like thunderclouds; thrust-out cock and flaming sword.

"Go find him," she whispered.

Cloud Angel by Susan Zutautas (CA)

We got the call, my sister and I, that dad had died shortly after we'd left the hospital for a few hours. Quickly we drove back to comfort mom and say our last goodbyes.

As we were leaving to drive home that night we looked up into the sky, and there before us was a brightly illuminated angel cloud floating by. A calmness came over both of us as we felt that this was dad saying his last goodbyes to us. He was now finally out of pain and at peace, after so many years of pain and suffering.

Angel's Light by Sherri Matthews (UK)

Gripping the steering wheel so hard that her knuckles turned white, Misty drove into the darkest corner of the car park and switched the engine off.

In the quiet and gripped by a sudden panic, she wondered why she had ever agreed to come on this blind date.

Walking across the dimly lit car park towards the pub's entrance, a bright light suddenly shot across the sky. Misty looked up at the pub sign, now mysteriously illuminated, as she stopped short: 'The Angel'.

A strange peace came over her then as she saw him walking towards her, smiling brightly.

Angels by Irene Waters (AU)

"Get up, Randolf. Time for school." Phaedra watched her son stir before going downstairs.

"Remind me why we sent Randolf to this school?" Her husband frowned as he looked over their son's report card.

"We wanted to give him a good start in life. We thought… Unicorn school would teach him how to properly channel his special powers. We wanted him to be an angel."

"Instead we've paid a fortune for the privilege of seeing him as an angel only if he gets chosen for the part in the Christmas play. They've created a unicorn with attitude and gun.

CHAPTER 7

Flash Fiction Challenge: In 99 words (no more, no less) include a story where "blue skies won't wait for you."

———————◆•◆•◆———————

Blue Skies Won't Wait for You by Susan Zutautas (CA)

Blue Skies Won't Wait for You
Oh my darling yes it's true
No matter how much you try
No matter how much you do
Blue Skies Won't Wait for You

You get up each morning
You work the day away
The chickens to be fed
The cows milked
Stalls mucked out
Repairs to be made
Farmhouse cleaned
Family to feed
The baby put to bed

Blue Skies Won't Wait for You
Remember this is what I said
Take some time for yourself my darling
Or life will pass you by in a flash
Blue Skies Won't Wait For You

➜➤

He's Gone by Larry LaForge (US)

"You need to tell him," Janice said to her husband Stan.

"It's not as bad as the last heart attack," Stan insisted. "He'll be discharged in a few days."

"Still. You have to make peace with your Dad. Why wait?"

After a sleepless night, Stan told Janice he was heading to the hospital.

Janice heard a familiar melody and realized Stan forgot his cell phone. She answered it while running out trying to catch him. "He's gone," she said into the phone as Stan's truck drove away.

Sadly, the caller from the hospital had the same message.

He's gone.

Goodbye by Pete Fanning (US)

They stood in the driveway avoiding eye contact. Their one-year relationship had raced from one chapter to the next — the night they met, their first date, moving in together—until it had caught up to the moment he had never allowed himself to fully believe would come. But she had to finish school. At 19, her life was just beginning, who was he to interfere?

Finally she looked up to him, a cloud of hope in her otherwise clear blue eyes. Then he said the two words that would haunt him for the rest of his life.

"Take care."

Blue Sky Freedom by Sherri Matthews (UK)

Catherine bristled. Breathing deeply, she stood up along with the others as the Bridal Chorus played.

"What's wrong?" whispered Steve without looking at her.

"Nothing!" she hissed. "I'm fine!"

Spoken vows scratched across Catherine's heart like shards of glass, her wounds fresh and deep.

Steve leaned in. "Blue skies won't wait for you, sweetheart, so if you want out, then get out. I'm not stopping you!"

Catherine stared at a single shaft of light beaming in through the stained glass window behind the vicar as he declared:

"I now pronounce you man and wife. You may kiss the bride!"

A Life-Changing Event by Ruchira Khanna (US)

Sam is being playful while looking at himself in the mirror.

Mom passes by his room to find him in such a state.

Walks in with her hands on her hips and a frown on her face.

Sam looks at her and quickly turns towards his papers.

Taking a deep breath, she strokes her hand over his head and says gently, "You can be comical all you want tomorrow evening after your significant and compelling event."

Pats his shoulder as if trying to make him understand, "Ought to be serious, Sam. The blue skies won't wait for you."

Blue Skies Won't Wait for You by Irene Waters (AU)

"Come on. It's a beautiful blue day. Let's have a picnic."

"No, I'm too busy. Let's go tomorrow. I'll enjoy myself then."

Grey skies with unrelenting rain met them the next day. "Should've gone on that picnic yesterday, love."

"We'll go as soon as it's fine."

Three days passed and there was still no sign of it abating.

Jack woke early the next day. A beautiful blue day. He prepared the picnic basket before taking in a cup of tea to Joan.

"Cuppa Joan." She stared back at him with unseeing eyes.

"Blue skies won't wait for you."

Blue Skies by Sarah Unsicker (US)

The dreary day was so different from the funeral sunshine. Cecilia could hardly recall it, her grief overpowering her ability to perceive, to live. She remembered her sister holding her up, moving her arms as if she were a life-sized doll. Cecilia had needed her lifelessness to bring him back to life. Instead, it had robbed her of her own life. In the depths of her grief, her daughter had grown up alone. Now Kate was gone. As Cecilia awoke to her reality, she understood what her mother had meant when she said, "blue skies won't wait for you."

Blue Skies Won't Wait For You by Amber Prince (US)

"It's time to go."

She watched the rain-drops collide into the window and race each other downwards. "Not today, please."

Her mother sighed. "If not today, when?"

"Another day."

They looked around the empty room, avoiding the blood-stained carpet, knowing that any other day was not an option. Her mother placed a hand on one of her bandaged arms. "You might not have another day."

She knew that it was time, but she was scared. Of what was to come. Of what had come to pass.

Her mother held out a hand. Together, they left her childhood room behind.

Blue Skies Won't Wait for You by Allison Mills (US)

Chelsea exhaled. Did she really have to pee? The window was dark.

She peeled back the quilt, sighing. The hand-hewn wooden planks under her feet creaked, the screen door echoing their complaints; the old Finnish sauna-turned-cabin was old.

But standing. That couldn't be said for the rest of the buildings on the Korhonen Homestead. The two-story house was mostly collapsed, the porch awning kissing the kitchen floor.

The outhouse was too far. Chelsea squatted over a stunted, killed-by-urine thistle in the yard beside one of the gnarled thorn apple trees. Relieved, she just couldn't wait for blue skies.

New Horizons by Geoff Le Pard (UK)

'We'll be in the car.' Paul and Penny, husband and daughter, walked outside.

Mary closed her eyes, imagining a life without folds and shadows. Without lawyers and email and unwanted relations. She picked up her coat. Scotland and a break. A chance to stop thinking, to let in some light.

Penny waved hard, almost as if the draught would pull Mary over. Paul pointed up. 'The blue skies won't wait forever.'

Mary slammed the front door. 'Blue skies?' She smiled. 'We're going to Scotland, not the Seychelles.'

'It's not the location. The blue sky is in your smile, love.'

CHAPTER 8

Flash Fiction Challenge: In 99 words (no more, no less) write a story about rare gems.

Rare Gems by Sarah Unsicker (US)

Bucket and shovel in hand, my boots carry me two miles to the beach. The sky is still dark; stars are fading, and the water reflects pink. "Pink in the morning, sailor take warning" is not only a saying, and I know a storm is brewing.

The wind blusters as I squat down. I return the first to the ground; the second is good. I pick my last as the tide reaches my boots. I walk home against the wind, the Eastern sky fully pink now. As I open the front door, the torrent arrives.

"Mom, clams again?"

The Fishing Boat by Larry LaForge (US)

Ed whooped; Edna screamed. They both knew what the $10,000 lottery winnings meant.

Ed had lusted after a 16-foot bass boat, modest by most standards but a yacht to him. "When you win the lottery, dear," Edna repeated annually at the boat show.

With winnings in hand, Ed checked his trailer hitch and headed to Bass Boat World.

Hours later, Edna noticed Ed's truck was back with nothing in tow.

Something on the table caught her eye. She opened the card.

"One rare gem deserves another."

A small box contained the diamond ring Ed couldn't afford 43 years ago.

Rare Gem by Rebecca Glaessner (AU)

A deep purple crystal warmed her hand. She searched, heart fluttering. A sea of people washing by, lives busy, unaware.

Eyes darting from face to face, she glanced from necklaces to clutched hands. She glimpsed an unfamiliar man, impressive with his suit and greying hair. Confused, he stared down at his palm.

She approached, dodging through the crowd. Her crystal growing warmer.

His eyes lifted and met hers. They locked.

She froze.

So you are the one? A deep voice rumbled in her mind, a soft smile sparkling in his eyes.

Smiling, she held her soul-stone to her heart.

Taking Stock by Geoff Le Pard (UK)

Mary let the last rays of the year's sun warm her face. Paul held her hand. 'Bit of an annus horribilis', he said.

She nodded.

'New year's resolutions?'

'Find this twin sister I'm meant to have.'

'She's probably dead. They'd have kept you together, surely?'

'Now maybe. Not back then.'

'Bury the hatchet with Rupert?'

Her loathsome half-brother. 'Maybe.'

Paul held out a box. 'I know it's early but twenty years married means platinum.'

She held up the ring, smiling. 'Grandma's?'

'Yes. The band was so worn I had the stones reset.'

Mary kissed her husband. 'My diamond geezer.'

Imperfect but Beautiful by Paula Moyer (US)

Jean looked at the ad and felt the tug of a vision. A needlepoint. She had not put needle to canvas in over 30 years. But she could just see it, framed, a gift for someone who had passed a milestone. She ordered the kit and began.

She ran out of yarn. Sigh — who does that skimpy Continental stitch anyway?

She ordered more. Even so, she ran out of red. Again. Substituted pink and orange in a corner with geometric shapes.

When she brought it home from the framers, she could not see where the substitution was. Good enough.

Uncut Gem by Norah Colvin (AU)

She examined the new arrival to assess the possible effects of integration into the existing collective. Would the group be enhanced or would this newcomer disrupt the established harmony?

From every angle the edges were rough and uneven. The years of obvious neglect obscured the potential from any but a trained eye.

Fortunately her eyes were keen. A bit of encouragement here, a little adjustment there, an opportunity to sparkle and display unique and positive attributes.

She smiled. Experience had shown what could be achieved with a little polish and gentle care.

"Welcome to our class, Marnie," she said.

Rare Gems by Irene Waters (AU)

"Dad, stop. You can't dig a mine under the house." Janie grabbed the pneumatic drill from Peter and pointed him towards the house.

When her father was out of earshot she said, "You have to put him in a home. The house'll fall down if he continues. He's demented"

"Once a mining engineer, always a mining engineer. He says he's looking for rare gems."

"No, Mum. He needs a nursing home."

"You're right, Janie. I'll do it today."

"Demented, you think." Talking to himself, Peter patted his back pocket. His escape route lay snuggly in the plastic bag he'd just excavated.

My Magic Compass by Pete Fanning (US)

I have this old compass. It's dull and dented and the needle is stuck. On the back is a crinkled print of Indian Head Mountain, a fading sunset behind clouds hardly distinguishable from the peeling edges of the sticker.

To a collector it's worthless, a trinket from a gift shop that found its way into my grandfather's pocket. And yet, it works beautifully.

It navigates my own faded memory, back to when the needle aligned and the picture was clear. It points to those fuzzy moments etched in the wrinkles of my childhood. It's magic, that compass, pure magic.

Rare Gems Flash Fiction by Anne Goodwin (UK)

"Call this Christmas?"

After a tough year, I'd wanted to make it special. It wasn't my fault our husky sled ride was cancelled and the aurora borealis refused to show. We had each other.

"I'm off to the bar."

I woke with a start, Pete snoring beside me. Grabbing my gown against the chill, I peeked through a gap in the curtains. The sky was a ballet of green and purple suspended above a stage of snow.

Next morning, he had a headache. I had the memory of a gem of a performance, choreographed for an audience of one.

Rare Gems Flash Fiction by Georgia Bell (CA)

She'd found the picture the other day. Rummaging through the box that held keepsakes she mostly forgot were important. She'd studied it for a moment and then tucked it into the pocket of her jeans.

But later, when the kids were in bed and her husband was watching the game, she poured herself a glass of wine and held it gently between her fingers.

His smile.

The way her hair had curled gently around her ears.

His hand resting on her elbow.

The look in her eyes. Excitement. Anticipation.

She exhaled and carefully tore it up into tiny pieces.

CHAPTER 9

Flash Fiction Challenge: In 99 words (no more, no less) write a story about disorientation.

Up is Down by Jeanne Belisle Lombardo (US)

He'd caught a good one, slipped into the swell right before it crested, paddled hard to keep with it, raced the vanguard foam till he felt it lift him, carry him on enormous blue shoulders, powerful, the sun blazing, the gulls screaming, the distant shouts spangling the air, the majestic length of the wave tunneling its way to the shore. Riding it! Flying the board of his body through it! Then a flinch. A tumble. A battering of bubbles. Tossed like flotsam. Limbs akimbo. Eyes stinging. Lungs exploding. Salt. Compression. Pumping to the surface. Hitting the sandy sea floor.

Disorientation in Haiti by Anne Goodwin (UK)

Some put their faith in gold, God, and governments; I thanked gravity for my anchor in this turbulent world. Friends and lovers might desert me, but Mother Earth was always there. April to October I went barefoot: pounding on asphalt, shuffling through sand or squelching mud between my toes, corporeally connected to solid ground.

I thought I'd gone mad when I heard the rumbling in her bowels. I never imagined the earth would betray me, let her surface crack like an egg. Soil in my mouth, grass in my hair, feet touching only air, I never dreamt I'd survive.

Birthday Party by Sarah Unsicker (US)

The air is dark, the music salty. Shoelaces glow; neon lights shine, but do not illuminate.

People huddle, but do not invite. People swarm everywhere, numerous as the chairs on wheels. The chairs are predictable. When moved, they slide. When spun, they turn. Spinning them with eyes closed blocks out the confusion of the bowling alley.

You carry an unwieldy sphere to the line, hold it between your spindly legs, and push it forward. Your muscles strain with the effort of coordination. Pins drop all around as your ball rolls to a stop in the middle of the lane.

Whiteout by Susan Zutautas (CA)

Hands clenched around the steering wheel, knuckles white, and heart pounding with fear.

Flurries were forecasted this afternoon but not total whiteouts.

I should have stayed at school.

Wanting desperately to pull over as I couldn't see a thing in front of me, I kept hearing a little voice in my head saying, "No one will see you and you'll get rear-ended for sure."

Suddenly I saw tail lights from another car and followed it until I could no longer see them.

Winds were strong, and I was fighting to keep my car on the road.

Whiteouts finally cleared.

Welcome to the Jungle by Sherri Matthews (UK)

"C'mon, Trudi, don't be a spoil-sport," whined Carla. "We'll have a blast!"

Trudi peered inside. "But it's late…"

Grabbing Trudi's hand, Carla marched her through the door as heads swivelled.

Trudi staggered across the room, strobe lights searing her vision, heavy base pounding in her chest. "I can't…see…" She reached for the nearest chair and missed, collapsing on the floor.

"What the hell, Jake. Why did you give her that pill?" Carla seethed as she dialled for the ambulance.

Jake looked down as Trudi vomited on his boots and passed out.

Restroom Signage by Larry LaForge (US)

He'd never had a Jell-O shot before. Now he's had at least one too many.

He heads down the narrow hallway toward the restrooms at The Chic Bar, keeping one arm on the wall for balance. At the end of the hall there are two metal doors, both labeled only with a fancy stick figure. He scratches his head. The figures look nearly identical, especially with his fuzzy vision. He turns his head sideways, but it doesn't help.

Decisions. Decisions.

With no time to waste, he shrugs his shoulders and proceeds.

Sudden, loud screams don't help his throbbing head.

Learning by Rebecca Glaessner (AU)

I'm holding tight, too tight, relax the hands, relax the back, breathe. It's okay.

Lights flash past. Eyes dart up, down, left, right, checking. They settle straight ahead for a moment, only to dart around again and again, keeping tabs on all surrounds.

Hands are gripping tighter again. Relax. Breathe.

So many things to focus on — perhaps too many things.

Breathe. Concentrate.

I can hear our little ones asleep behind us.

Look up. Focus. How fast? Who's behind? Where do I need to go?

I flick the indicator, looking left. I merge.

I wonder when the confidence will come.

The Results are in! by Ruchira Khanna (US)

"Harry, the results are in!" shouted Mom while holding the newspaper in one hand and giving a hard push to the sleepy head.

"So what do I do?" came a torpid reply.

Confused, Mom stared at him in bewilderment.

Gulped in order to control her temper, and tried to speak softly while avoiding to break off. "Well, give me your number, and let's check if you cleared."

"Sure, first let me catch up on my sleep. The results are here to stay!"

Perplexed, Mom was astonished and wondered where is the element of excitement located in her son.

Not All Houses Are Homes by Roger Shipp (US)

My book bag — Old Navy, camouflage — was in the back: four sets of clothes, sneakers, and a set of tightly, rubber-band-bound envelopes. My life: assorted letters, and two photographs, from the last three years. That was everything, except for my Riptunes MP3. I was listening to Bastille "Things We Lost" for the umpteenth time.

We were watching for a large white SUV driven by a balding, older man and his grey-haired wife.

My ninth home: a new family — this one much older. I was ready: eyes — dry, dulled, unexpressive. New starts aren't what they are cracked up to be.

When Memory Lane Turns into a Stroll by C. Jai Ferry (US)

Stagnant cologne emanated from her clothes, suffocating her in the tiny kitchen. Remnants of a late-night burger were piled on the unfamiliar Formica counter. Her stomach lurched, belching up bubbles laced with last night's Stolichnaya, and she wiped crusty mascara from her eyes. Her head pulsated in a dull thud while flashing visions of popcorn ceilings and her red lace bra and her keys clanging against cold bathroom tile. She shuffled from the kitchen just as she heard a door handle click open. She froze, pleading with her synapses to connect the dots. Just whose apartment was she in?

CHAPTER 10

Flash Fiction Challenge: In 99 words (no more, no less) craft a multiverse situation, setting, or character(s).

Clone Magic by Norah Colvin (AU)

All night Leone had huddled in line. She was sleepless with excitement, waiting for the release.

Now she had them! Clone pills!

"Take one with water. Cloning occurs in 30 minutes and lasts 24 hours."

Leone swallowed one tablet, then another and another, ignoring the small print: "Do not take multiple tablets. Effects are unpredictable."

When three clones appeared she instructed:

"1. Clean the house. 2. Exercise. 3. Weed the garden."

She flopped on the couch. "Now to read."

But their hands grabbed for her book, pulling her hair and clawing her eyes.

"Me read! Me read! Me read!"

Fast Forward by Susan Zutautas (CA)

I awoke to my alarm going off; I stretched and rubbed my glued eyes. In disbelief I looked around at my bedroom, which did not look anything like it did when I went to sleep.

The room had expanded; new furnishings, wall covering, and a master suite were all in my sight.

What the hell was going on?

I could hear voices coming from the kitchen but they didn't sound familiar. What I saw when entering the room shocked me. Standing by the island were two twin girls and an older version of my son.

Mom you're awake…

The Crosswalk by Sarah Unsicker (US)

We wait together for the walk signal. She is dressed smartly for court; I push a twin stroller in marker-stained jeans. I ask what kind of hearing she has.

"Pretrial," she says, "a bail hearing." I recognize the client from her description. He was homeless and couldn't afford health care. She looks as nervous as I remember feeling.

"You'll do fine," I say, confidently. This case will start her short but successful career.

My gaze rests on the pearls my husband gave me, on the suit that hangs in my closet. I again contemplate the cost of child care.

Shift Worker by Paula Moyer (US)

Two months after they started dating, Jean met Charlie's family. His father worked at the gypsum plant, or "the rock crusher," with rotating shifts. Her own parents worked bankers' hours.

One night after dinner, the phone rang. Charlie bolted from the couch in his stocking feet, slid into the kitchen. He grabbed the phone before the second ring.

"Hello?" he whispered.

Pause.

"Oh, good evening. Could you call back tomorrow? Daddy's asleep." All whispered.

Part of Charlie's world came into focus.

Work hours dictated sleep hours. Loud talk, ringing phones — toxic when his dad's workday started at 3 a.m.

Cosmostology by Larry LaForge (US)

"I've always been interested in cosmology," Maria yapped as she curled her customer's hair.

"You mean cosmetology, dear," Mrs. Krieger said with a condescending smile.

The hairdresser didn't respond.

Maria saw far more than bristly hair. She saw an entire universe on top of the elderly woman's head — a cosmos of follicles alive and interacting, some in concert and some in protest. She saw growth and decline. No matter the intervention, Maria knew the natural order would ultimately prevail.

"Thanks," Maria said upon receiving a generous tip.

Mrs. Albertson was next. Maria smiled, anticipating the battle of the bangs.

Worlds Apart by Pete Fanning (US)

It was August hot in October, humid and sticky without the faintest hope of a breeze. Dad wiped his brow, taking a nauseating drag of his cigarette as we sat in the truck, waiting for Mom.

A shiny car edged into the space beside us, its thumping music drowning the tinny sounds of Dad's country station. I peeked out as the mother unbuckled her child, the beads in her hair clicking and clacking with the movement. Dad exhaled purposely as he stubbed out his cigarette beside the pickets of brown butts in the ashtray.

"I just don't understand them."

The Duchess, The Daughter by Sarah Brentyn (US)

I woke up at home.

My parents called lots of people. They cried and hugged me too much.

They said it had been three weeks since I disappeared.

I told them about the bears who declared war on the humans. The hedgehogs who made me laugh despite what was happening in the world. My wedding to the duke. My baby girl who I missed so much it hurt.

Now I sit in the place where Mommy and Daddy visit me. The place where people give me pills with my morning pancakes. The place where I'm six years old again.

Naming Wild Bill by Charli Mills (US)

Hickok awoke to distant drumming. Since his release in matters concerning the shooting of Cob McCanless, he'd joined the Union Army as a civilian scout. Alone in the muggy backwoods of southern Missouri this nightly interruption continued. Soon the child on horseback would gallop past. A girl with auburn hair like his, wearing strange clothes the color of southwest turquoise. Each night she grew older until she drew up her horse above his bedroll, fully grown. She leveled a queer black gun at him, saying, "Wild Bill, you shot my kin!"

No one had ever called him that before.

Every Mirror Tells a Story by Geoff Le Pard (UK)

Mary hated herself for her indifference to Angela, her late father's mistress. She wanted to hate her but felt empty.

In her father's study she stood in front of the mirror, staring at the reflection of his picture. 'Why?'

Water ran down the mirror, like tears distorting his face. His lips moved. 'I'm so sorry.'

Peter pushed through the miasma that separated his world from Mary's, willing her to understand. They'd told him it would take all his courage, all his strength to make the bridge. If only he had had found the courage and strength before he died.

Multiverse Flash by Irene Waters (AU)

John jumped from the bridge without giving a second glance back. The swirling river below engulfed him, taking him into the dark depths. A crack of light appeared along with a voice whispering, "Stay away from the light," but the current propelled him toward it.

Caught in an eddy he hurtled through the void and suddenly aware of the sun warming his now naked flesh he saw he lay in a verdant field. Rising, he headed towards the sun uncertain where he should be headed. Thundering past, the unicorns beckoned.

"Blast. Last time I landed in Paris with Hemingway."

CHAPTER 11

Flash Fiction Challenge: In 99 words (no more, no less) write a story that includes a river and a person.

—————•◆•————

New Waters, New Home by Paula Moyer (US)

Oklahoma rivers run dry during a drought. When crossing a river on a highway bridge, Jean had always seen the river's path below like open lacework over a sandy bed. But here she was with her parents, at the first I-35 rest area across the Iowa border into Minnesota.

She stood at the window in the welcome center and looked down the hill at the body of water below. River or creek? She didn't know — what she did know was this: The Minnesota creeks looked almost like oceans compared to the Oklahoma rivers.

She also knew: She was home.

River Rat by Sherri Matthews (UK)

The small, wooden boats lined the riverbank in a neat row exactly as Ken remembered, waiting for hire by visitors suddenly overcome with the urge to take to the water.

Idiots.

Ken ambled along the path, keeping one eye on the river. Then he saw it and stopped short: the very spot where he and Muriel had picnicked before she had asked him to take her boating.

Of course, darling, he had said, knowing she couldn't swim. Faking an accident on the river would be easy.

Ken jolted awake, his hopes dashed as Muriel snored peacefully by his side.

A Wish Turned into a Reality! by Ruchira Khanna (US)

Kate is toddling in the stream and humming along as the cold temperature is rejuvenating her from the daily grind.

"Are you done?" came an urgent inquiry. "Can we go to see that waterfall around the corner?"

She turned towards him. "Nah! not yet. I am loving it to such an extent that I wanna merge into it," replied with a giggle.

Just then a loud shriek was heard, followed by panic, agitation, and soon the voice got drained off.

Her companion was devastated to see her float away. Jeez! Nature was quick to say Amen to her thoughts."

Baptism by Fire and Water by Charli Mills (US)

Lucinda belly-crawled to the edge of the creek. Behind her she heard the metal of her DC-10 bulldozer ping in the heat. Soon the roaring wildfire would engulf the equipment meant to build a barrier. Trees exploded and flaming pitch arced above black smoke like holiday fireworks. The heat was blistering even as Lucinda waded into the creek, dipping her entire head and body in the water. Two moose stared at her, a wall of flame behind them. She whispered a silent prayer. Forgive us our trespasses against this land. Thank you for the water. May it be enough.

Attempt #73 by Pete Fanning (US)

"Here's one!" Carla squealed, holding up a squirming salamander with two fingers.

Emmit looked it over closely. "That's a good one."

At dinner they sat up straight and proper, elbows off the table. The katydids wound down the evening. They exchanged glances, stifling giggles. A fuzz of creek sand still covered their feet.

"What did you two do today?" their father asked.

"Nothing," they said in unison.

Emmit nodded. Carla whimpered. Her father leaned over to look at her finger. Emmit worked quickly, dropping the salamander into her glass just before his stepmother took her seat at the table.

River & Person Flash Fiction by Anne Goodwin (UK)

The tinkle of running water signalled we'd strayed from our route. By a long stretch. Emerging from the trees, I snatched the map from his hand, struggling to match the pattern of coloured lines with the landscape up ahead. He sat on a rock and bent to unknot the laces of his boots. "We haven't time to hang about," I said. The sun already sat low in the sky.

"Shush!"

Anger gripped me, until I looked where he was pointing. On a branch overhanging the river perched a kingfisher, regal in its electric-blue coat. Worth the detour, after all.

Revival by Rebecca Glaessner (AU)

She crashed through the underbrush, branches whipping bare skin. Lifeblood dripped from scratches, soaking the soil, eventually feeding those with which she shared her homes. Heart pounding, she pushed on.

The creatures gained ground.

She clambered out of the tree-line into deep, rushing water and waited...

He conquered the treetops, branch by branch. The creatures would watch in awe, though never catch him. He spotted the cascading water.

A shot rang as he dove over the edge, freefall...

Cool water enveloped the pair as they embraced, panting, washing away their exhaustion and carrying them on toward a new home.

Reunited... One More Chance? by Roger Shipp (US)

Side by side. Each in his own world.

Two poles purposefully pointed toward the ever-popping ripples in the fresh water pond.

A sharp tug. Another. And it's gone.

One — a runaway at fifteen who has returned home. The other — a fragile, ninety-year-old...lost in macular degeneration. Together now, but separated by forty years and fifteen feet.

Memories. A father tiptoeing in for a look at his son before work... Careful not to awaken him. A son sneaking home from being out all night...exhausted.

Both — blinded by memories of years never encountered.

A sharp tug. Another. And it's gone.

Stono Ferry by Larry LaForge (US)

"Dude, let's go. The group behind us is waiting."

Clayton's mind wasn't on the golf game he was losing to his partners. Instead, he stared intently at the plaque on the historic Stono River alongside the course.

He seemed mesmerized by events described on June 20, 1779. British troops approached Charleston. Ragged Patriot militia tried to hold them off at this ferry crossing. Lives were lost in the pursuit of liberties Clayton takes for granted every day.

His struggling golf game suddenly seemed ridiculously trivial.

"Coming," Clayton said, slowly walking away with his head still turned toward the river.

Red River by Irene Waters (AU)

"We've got to pull together to get through before the gate closes," Ruby yelled to Luke.

"One, two, three. Pull!" They continued upstream and pulled together at each gate.

"This is the last one. Hold on tight. You okay? You look blue, Ruby."

She nodded, breathless. "A little tired." Suddenly they plummeted down a Niagara-style drop into the swirling cavern below only to be pumped at speed along a new river which wound through the lush region of alveoli. As they passed, Ruby smiled, feeling her energy return. "I'm ready for the next run," she said, her colour returned.

CHAPTER 12

Flash Fiction Challenge: In 99 words (no more, no less) write a story that includes a fantastical element or creature.

Conservation by Lisa Reiter (UK)

It was hot but the door was closed. She snuck up to peek through a gap. She'd not been allowed to the barn since the birth, but Mother was distracted with Tommy.

She'd heard the grinder going. The horses were stamping and whinnying just like when there was a fire in the hayloft. Her father and the men were holding the newborn while the blacksmith seemed to be branding its bleeding head.

A shout — she'd been seen! Father rushed to get her. Gently he said:

"You mustn't tell anyone — there are bad people trying to wipe out the unicorns."

The Scaly Curse by Amber Prince (US)

The wind whipped her face as they soared across the night sky. She leaned forward, resting her face against the worn scales that made up his body. Their time together was coming to an end, they could both feel the changes in the air.

They were only given one night a year, as this was their curse. He wasn't even granted his old human form to be able to hold her tight. This is how they would share their love until one died or one forgot the other.

But she didn't care. The dragon was her father after all.

Dog Days and Phoenix Nights by Geoff Le Pard (UK)

It was morphogenesis; Milton was in flames but not in pain. Peter smiled. What next for the Staffie?

'He's smiling, Mum.'

'It's the sun. When they turn Grandpa to the window, it looks like he's smiling.' Mary slipped past the bleeping machines. 'Here, I'll move this.'

A horn grew from Milton's head; Peter knew now. A unicorn. The flames engulfed the dog, leaving the horn to point skywards. Peter felt happy at last.

'There.' Mary pulled the drip stand from the window so its shadow cut across Peter's face. 'I wish he'd give us a sign.'

'He's peaceful, Mum.'

The Patrick Cat by Jeanne Belisle Lombardo (US)

The rain stopped. She stepped through to the patio, drank in the scent of quenched earth and creosote, and then moved to the Palo Verde tree.

Her hand on the smooth, green bark, she looked east. A rainbow crowned Fire Rock Mountain.

Then she noticed it, the chain, hanging free from a bough. The terracotta winged cat that Patrick had given her was gone.

She toed the earth. "Where are you, Patrick?" she whispered. "Don't die on me again."

A rustle near the rosemary. A cat the color of clay pawed the air. "Meer," it said. And took flight.

The Secret Stall by Charli Mills (US)

"I don't wanna pick blackberries. They got too many thorns." Libby stuck her throbbing thumb in her mouth.

"Look, Libby's a baby." Her brother Joe pointed and their cousins laughed. Libby headed to the barn. The cat was nicer than these five boys.

"Here kitty…" She could hear boy-chatter across the yard. It was dark inside. A shuffle sounded from behind the farm tractor. Careful not to trip over tools, Libby made her way to the back where a glow in the stall revealed a shining horn.

It was attached to a unicorn sleeping on a pile of quilts.

The Unicorn by Irene Waters (AU)

Jack hurt. Crammed in the barrow like a foetus in the womb he screamed but his taped mouth ensured silence and made breathing difficult. His ears hurt from the high-pitched squeak of the wheelbarrow. A new sound, barely audible at first, came softly, a tinkling of tiny bells blown in the breeze. His breathing slowed as the chimes calmed him. He felt he was no longer alone with the barrow man but dismissed the occasional glimpses of the white, one-horned horse as pure fantasy. He had lost track of time. He no longer knew in what realm he travelled.

Unicorn Knights by Norah Colvin (AU)

She sat on the bed and looked around. Funny how some things don't change.

They had left it untouched for all those years since her escape, waiting for her return. But she never did. Never could. Until now.

"You should," she was told.

"Make peace."

"Let it go."

It didn't look so scary now. They were both gone. She was grown.

Sunlight glinted on the unicorn. It had faded but waited still, on the night-table, for their nocturnal escapades away from cruel reality.

She fingered it for a moment, remembering. Then dumped it in the wastebasket.

"Sell!" she said.

Flash Fiction by Anne Goodwin (UK)

He woke with the sun and staggered to his feet. He felt clumsy, heavy head and throbbing forehead echoing the antics of the night before. The music. The dancing. The drugs.

He tried to join his siblings, but they showed him their backs. He trotted towards his mother, but his aunts barred his way.

Thirst raging in his throat, he cantered to the pool. Bending to drink, he caught his reflection: hooves; fetlocks; knees; chest; muzzle. Yet no longer a horse: projecting from his forehead, a huge horn spiralled to a point. He'd be living as a unicorn now.

Rainbows and Unicorns by Georgia Bell (CA)

The woman smiled, faint lines around her eyes crinkling as she shook her head. "God, was I ever that young?"

The girl stepped back into the shadows, unsure and uncertain. "Who are you?"

The woman extended her hand. "Come with me," she said. "There's not much time."

"For what?" The girl moved into the sun again, drawn towards this woman whose hair sparkled with the same golden sheen as hers.

"To make things different," she said. "To make things right."

"How do you know which is which?" the girl asked.

"You don't," the woman said. "That's why I'm here."

A Knight in Plastic Armor by Pete Fanning (US)

Dylan trudged home, his sword clicking on the sidewalk behind his steps. Sir Galahad followed obediently, his dented cardboard horn still affixed to his head.

Dylan knew naught that a unicorn would incite such howls of laughter from the knights of the picnic table — a most shameful lot indeed, he thought piteously. Therewith Galahad barked and Dylan spun around to find Amelia, Sir Derrick's older sister.

"Dylan." She approached, shining with…well she was on the phone. "Here, you forgot your cake." Galahad nosed the chocolate frosted offering.

"Thank you, me lady, thou–"

"Come on, Dylan. Don't push it."

PART 2: A NEW FLASH FICTION CHALLENGE

Note from the Editor, Sarah Brentyn:

For newbies who hadn't contributed to the weekly flash, I devised a scheme to get them into the anthology with a fun exercise. These fabulous writers were up for the challenge.

Our Series Editor, Charli Mills, took the challenge, too.

I gave them little warning: three words and three days to come up with a 99-word flash. They received the following email:

Okay, fellow flashers. Here's how this challenge is going to work. (I know what I'm doing—trust me.)

1. *I will send each of you an email with the same three words (guard them with your life).*
2. *You must incorporate all three words in your flash (yes, all three).*
3. *Your flash must be exactly 99 words (not including title).*
4. *Once you receive the three-word prompt, you have three days to write it (you can thank my husband for that — I was going to give you one day).*

That's it! Sound easy? Good. (I know. It really doesn't. But it's fun and will create some truly unique and fantastic flashes.)

Let me know if you're still interested in writing (and I really hope you are). Please send an email saying, "Challenge Accepted!"

Once they had accepted, they got this:

Thanks for joining in! Here are the three words:

Lamp
Tree
Juice

These must be included in your flash but can be any form of the word (tree/trees/treetop, juice/juicing/juicer/juicy, etc.).

You have three days. Good luck. This message will self-destruct in 5 seconds.

And here, lovely readers, is what they came up with. Enjoy the flash. It's awesome. And do give this challenge a try. It's great fun.

Industrious Evolution by JulesPaige (US)

Hamm spit the juice of his chewing tobacco by the base of the old oak tree that had been struck by lightning almost at the edge of the back forty. His lamp flickering low as he bent on one knee to brush away the debris that had collected at the base of Cora's gravestone.

The children all grown, wanted nothing to do with the farm. Hamm wondered what would become of his private family cemetery. Rascal his dog rested his head on his master's bent leg. The Ortegas were grateful for the work. Senora O cooked just fine, too.

First Kiss by Sacha Black (UK)

The lamp hung from the tree branch, swaying in the evening breeze. It cast an eerie glow over the sleeping bags. Tom lay across from me, sipping juice.

Tingles erupted in my stomach as I realised he was staring at me. My cheeks flamed. I'd spent a week desperate for him to notice me, but now he had, it terrified me.

He scanned the sleeping lumps. When he was sure they were snoozing he whispered, "You're beautiful. But you're blind! I've been after you all week."

Then he leant in, pressed his lips to mine, and everything else disappeared.

The Guitar Man by Kate Spencer (CA)

Jennifer found herself humming along with the juicy fruit jingle while checking out the dress in the storefront window. There was something familiar about these cadences. She knew a person who liked to play these… It couldn't be him, could it?

She turned and stared down the busy street.

There he was, sitting on a stool under a sidewalk tree, strumming his guitar. He was bundled up in a parka, his face hidden from view. Jennifer ran toward him.

She stopped breathless beside his kerosene lamp. He looked up. Her eyes swelled with tears as she recognized her Dad.

The Matrilineal Ritual by C. Jai Ferry (US)

Charcoaled cottonwood trees towered over her. The sweet aroma of her great-grandmother's lilac bushes embraced her while God flipped on the stars' lights one by one. When she was young and all-knowing, she'd complained to her mother of the lack of street lamps in the country. Now she leaned back in her mother's rocker, rattling the ice in her amber glass as she finished off her grandmother's recipe: one part orange juice and nine parts vodka. She'd finally exchanged omniscience for wisdom, making peace with nature's shadowy silhouettes, but her mother was too long gone to celebrate with her.

The Deposition by Urszula Humienik (Poland)

I remember that time well; I was on a juice cleanse and felt so clearheaded, although something palpable was missing.

Hazel and I'd planned to meet by a lamppost near her home. We met there often. That afternoon we'd intended to go to the bookstore cafe to meet with friends. That was the plan.

When we met, Hazel told me we had to take a small detour first. She took me to a large meadow, which led to a forest, and then a clearing somewhere in the middle, with a giant oak tree.

She touched the tree and disappeared.

Treehouse Memories by Christina Rose (US)

The soprano hum of cicadas and the staccato chirp of crickets enveloped their fantasy world in nature's symphony. High in the treehouse, the young sisters spread their soft blankets, creating a cozy nest of innocent delight.

Mother packed treats for the night: sandwiches, juice boxes, cookies. Quickly devoured, fingers sticky with sweet, mouths ringed with childhood bliss; nourishment for a night of ghost stories and truth or dare.

Moths gathered around the soft, golden glow of the crackling lamp. Flapping wings cast glimmering shadows across the mounds of downy pillows, the fort lulling them into an enchanting childhood slumber.

Secret Santa by Luccia Gray (Spain)

I took the empty glass of apple juice from the nightstand, turned off the lamp, and kissed Sally goodnight.

"Will Father Christmas find the tree in the dark, mummy?"

"I'm sure he will."

"Will he find our new home?"

I wanted Sally to have a normal holiday in spite of moving to the safe-house, where her father couldn't find us.

"Of course."

She smiled. "Daddy told me the truth. He's dressing up as Father Christmas and bringing our presents."

A shiver travelled up my spine, prickling the hairs on my neck.

"Ho, ho, ho! Who's been hiding from Santa?"

Alice by Sarrah J. Woods (US)

Alice ignores the blaring television across from her bed and looks out the window. The crab apple tree's branches are now bare except for a few berries, which a family of plump robins snacks on by the last light of sunset.

Her own family hasn't visited in months, but she understands. Their lives are full. Hers once was too.

An orderly comes in and switches on the lamp. "And how are we today?" he bellows. He knows, of course, that Alice can't talk.

But oh, he'll never suspect what hard-learned truths and juicy secrets are buried inside her mind.

Driftwood by Anthony Amore (US)

Since the tsunami he'd taken to carrying at least one heavy duty trash bag on his daily walks along the beach. Finding beer cans and juice bottles was never unusual — that was, until the beer cans and juice bottles with Japanese labels began bobbing along the water's edge. Lamps and toasters surfaced too. He imagined the items weren't random solitary castaways but gathered contents of one person's life, order from the chaos. This romantic notion provided comfort until the day his dog nosed at something buried beneath a tree branch, a blue Converse hi-top sneaker holding a severed foot.

The Last Sip by Charli Mills (US)

Marta fingered the grooved Fresnel lens, the lighthouse's massive lamp. She could light it, but who'd see the beacon? No ship dared Lake Superior once ice began to stack on shore. Fritz never returned. She'd nibbled the last smoked whitefish. Finished the blueberry jam. Marta contemplated the silver juice floating the lens.

Amy pointed past the birch tree. "A lady, Mama!" The park ranger and his tour glanced up at the State Park Lighthouse. Nothing but an old Fresnel lens.

The ranger continued. "One mystery was the disappearance of the last light-keeper and the death of his poisoned wife."

PART 3: EXPANDED FLASH is in response to those 99-word stories that hold anticipation of more to come. Often readers want to know more about the stories or characters introduced in 99 words. Five of the Rough Writers expanded original 99-word stories into longer versions, each under 2,000 words. This process exemplifies how flash fiction can be the seed for a more developed story. It's a tool writers can use to come up with new work.

First, the 99-word originals:

Normandy by Pete Fanning (US)

My room was busy today.

My son came with his family.

The waves of names crashed down on me, only I was back on that beach, where I'd held my best friend in his final moments as a hail of mortar and gunfire rained down on us, the taste of salt water and iron on my lips.

But I'm a stranger to them.

Ellie would have handled this better, she'd always been able to smooth the edges. Oh my sweet Ellie! Her face had faded in the prison that was my own mind.

I was alone on that beach.

Country House Hotel by Anne Goodwin (UK)

Tyres crunching on gravel snapped Mum out of her doze. "Oh, my!"

The grand house loomed ahead. "Do you recognise it?" said my sister.

I parked by the porticoed entrance. Beyond banks of rhododendrons, the lake shimmered. My sister hopped out and opened Mum's door. "Bet you're itching to explore."

Mum stayed put.

"How about tea first?"

Mum didn't budge.

My sister took her wrinkled hand. "It's where you were evacuated, remember?" Mum's tales of wartime escapades were embedded in our childhoods. "It's a hotel now." This mini-break, the perfect birthday treat.

Mum was almost retching. "No, please, no."

Unfolding Drama by Geoff Le Pard (UK)

'If you care, be there.'

She held out the note.

'Check-in is two hours before the flight.'

He glanced down. City Airport. BA desk. Friday.

He knew it was pointless, calling, discussing it. Too much water had been passed, as Sam Goldwyn said.

Friday. He smoothed the note and smiled. Two hours before; his timing was perfect. He approached the desk. 'Flight 265?'

The attendant pointed at the plane taking off. The note said 4.20. He was on time. He narrowed his eyes. In the crease, a faint vertical line, like a middle finger, stared back at him. 14.20.

Crimson Sunset by Ann Edall-Robson (CA)

Crimson reds, smatterings of yellow, fading into the blackening sky. Standing in the open door of the log house he watched the sun set over the foothills.

It had not been many years since he'd brought her here as his wife. Hoping she would love the rolling hills and the house he had built for her. She never said it, but he knew she was unhappy.

He would stay on. This had always been his home and in his heart it would always be hers, too.

As he turned to go in, he heard her voice call his name.

The Journal by Georgia Bell (CA)

She started and ended the same way. Fragile, dependent, full of curiosity and wonder. In between her first and last breath, she learned to love, to hate, to be brave, to forgive. She learned that grief made her life more meaningful and taking risks is what kept her alive. She became stronger than she thought she'd ever be, and softer too. Able to soothe the glorious, savage beast her body brought into the world. She watched the tiny boy grow into a man she loved as much as the one she had lost. She had lived. She was proud.

CHAPTER 1

Normandy by Pete Fanning (US)

———◆•◆•◆———

My room was busy today. My son Tate with his kids, his oldest with a kid of her own. Waves of names crashed down on me. Noise and commotion, voices talking over the top of each other. I could only nod along, lost in the speed of things as they went about their conversations.

When the chatter died down and they took to their phones, I knew it was almost over. Tate busied himself with the room, the kids, straightening pictures on the wall, so that I never got a moment alone with him. A stiff handshake on the way out was our only link, a cold squeeze to acknowledge blood and circumstance.

I don't know this man who is my son. Hardly better than his brother who managed only a few precious minutes of life. And I was supposed to change all of that — I said that I would. But I haven't the slightest clue how to go about it.

Elsie handled these affairs. I was left to nod and grunt. She'd known all the names, the birthdates, and the graduations. She cooked glorious dinners and baked cookies for the grandchildren, knitting us all together with her kindness and spirit.

When she fell ill they were devastated. Horrified glances fell to me, as though I didn't know that it was a rotten deal, that it should have been me. It would have been easier that way, not that Elsie thought so. She was strong, and as always, working with all she could to her last days trying to connect me to them. So now we shake hands.

When Tate and the kids were gone, a hushed relief came over me. Oh, my sweet Elsie. I promised that I could do it. That I would have an honest talk with him and get to know my grandchildren. It's the only lie I've ever told her.

Perhaps it's because I'm more acquainted with the dead than the living. I stepped over it, through it, slung it over my back on that beach so many years ago.

I'd held my best friend in his final moments, as a hail of mortar and gunfire came raining down on us, the taste of salt water and iron on my lips.

Now my lips were cracked and chapped as I looked over the bombardment of trash. Wrappers, diapers, soda bottles between the dented pillows on the couch. The trail of the disposables.

Oh Francis. You've become such an old crank.

At the sound of her voice I looked to her picture in the oval frame. Elsie at the fair, the night we met. Posed with her head back and her arms to her sides, the photograph so worn and riddled with scratches but seared into my mind. I knew then she was my light. With Elsie the ocean never turned on me. The sand was always clean. Soft and forgiving. Her laughter obliterated the groans and cries of men on their way out of life.

Why didn't you talk to him? He wants you to talk to him.

"What should I say, Elsie?"

Nurse Vickie stood before me. "Good afternoon, Francis. Did your family come today?"

Her eyes fell to Elsie in my grip. I returned her picture to the shelf, wondering what Vickie had heard or how much I'd said. If all the old widows and widowers talked to their spouses.

"Do you need some time before dinner?"

Dinner. We'd just had lunch. Nurse Vickie's eyes were wide and caring. She's easily my favorite staff nurse at Willows, one of the few who doesn't treat me like a toddler who'd pissed himself. "I'll come back after I make my rounds. You need anything, sweetie?"

I needed to be in a picture frame — shown off in a photo album instead of peeked at like a stranger. Spoke about in the past tense instead of the present. But no, I didn't need any apple juice.

When Vickie was gone I took the picture again, traced Elsie's youthful face with a hooked finger. How long had it been, five years? What did it matter?

I rose, finding socks and fighting to get them on my curled feet. I peeled off the elastic, yanked my real pants up, and clasped my suspenders. When I did, my nose conjured up a rosy fragrance that sent me back forty years. A flicker of Elsie at the mirror, Glenn Miller humming over the room. In a blink it ended, and I found my overcoat and made my way. But she wasn't finished with me.

Francis, no. Not yet.

Her hand fell on mine, like an amputee feels an itch. I stopped with my buttons and closed my eyes. Went back for her picture. Then I fixed my hat and walked right out of my door, charging down the hallway for the side door. With some commotion at the front desk, and all the fuss about the storm sweeping in, I simply slid out without notice.

The sky was milky gray, I pulled my coat tight against the biting wind and patted an empty back pocket as I thought about getting flowers. An old habit from a past life.

The bus wrenched to a stop. Cars whipped past the bus stop without warning. I hobbled aboard, my hip sending a blast of panic down my leg as I shuffled to a seat, winded and wincing and cursing my mind for overstaying its welcome. My body was an old vessel, one that could never walk the seven blocks to the cemetery.

When we started forward I was on that boat, with fifty other saps about to take fire. When that ramp came down I knew it was over for me. For all of us. I wasn't yet twenty and I'd kissed Elsie's picture a thousand times. I'd spoken to it then as I did now, my shield in a hail of iron and steel.

The bus doors opened. I crossed the street as I'd charged the shore, my gaze focused on the wrought iron fencing, the statues, so brave and stoic, unmoved by the years. I trudged through the gates as the first snowflake hit my cheek.

Inside those grounds my breathing returned to normal. A few lonely birds perched on stones. My pace slowed, and it occurred to me that I no longer remembered Elsie's funeral. Who spoke or what wonderful things were said about the woman I loved more than anything on this forsaken planet.

Our gravestone lay somewhere up the hill. Slipping through the dust I was sure as the moon that my feet would take me to her. Through the barrage of snowflakes that blurred the landscape, touched my shoulders, muted the world of sound. Of all the things that had slipped my memory, the ring of gunfire and the groan of death were not among them. The cries of my fellow brothers, the bloodstained sand. It held my soul in its grasp to this day.

I stumbled upon her. Around the naked oaks, just past the weeping angel. I wiped clean our slab of remembrance.

Elsie Jean Pollard 1926-2011

Francis T. Pollard 1925-

The dirt was unforgiving on my knees. My hands melted the new snow but did little to loosen the hardened soil of my own burial plot.

I'd failed us. I'd failed my family. Drowned in blood red waters where I'd defended my country only to lose touch with my countrymen. My son's cold hand still in my grip. Without Elsie I was all alone on that beach, taking breaths I no longer wished to take.

"I'm sorry, dear. I'm sorry I never came out of it."

The snow insulated those last minutes. Cold at first touch, then heavy and warm, like blood filling a wound. It covered a lifetime of horrors — war, Elsie in labor, a dying son's screams, a living son's resentment — like sand on the beach. I curled up next to my Elsie, using my unfinished marker for a pillow, closing my eyes as she whispered in my ear.

It's okay, Francis. It's okay.

CHAPTER 2

Country House Hotel by Anne Goodwin (UK)

———————◆◆◆———————

Des would've preferred to meet up at the hotel, but Bev was adamant. "It won't be the same if we don't travel together." He could've pointed out it wouldn't be the same anyway without Dad, but Bev could get stroppy when she was thwarted and the last thing their mother needed was them squabbling like a couple of kids.

It would have been strange driving past the hotel turnoff on the way up north, so Des took the train. Despite the inconvenience of an early start, he enjoyed the journey, sifting through the morning paper over a not-too-dreadful coffee and a breakfast baguette.

The old house looked smaller than he remembered. Even with the double-glazed windows and block-paved driveway, the place seemed frozen in the 1970s, and Des with it. He gave the taxi driver an extra-large tip, but it didn't make him feel any bigger than the boy who'd grown up here.

Bev answered the door. He dropped his bag and they hugged awkwardly in the cramped hallway, both pretending they'd have embraced more elegantly had there been more space. As his sister pushed off towards the kitchen to make him a cup of tea, he wondered if she'd had that old-fashioned smell of Parma violets the last time he'd seen her and whether her hair had been such an unnatural shade of red.

His mother was halfway up from her chair when he joined her in the lounge, like a wind-up toy that needed an extra turn of the handle to complete its routine. Des hugged her as clumsily as he'd hugged his sister, but this time it served a purpose: helping her to her feet and back to her seat.

He positioned himself on the end of the sofa, almost exactly as he'd sat as a boy on another sofa to watch TV. "You're looking well," he told his mother, his manufactured cheerfulness covering the shock and embarrassment at how wrinkled and gaunt she'd become since the funeral only two months before.

Bev brought his tea and commandeered the other end of the sofa. Des sipped from the china cup. "No one else having one?"

His mother looked hopefully across at Bev, but she shook her head. "Better not. Don't want to have to stop to spend a penny on the way there."

Des watched his mother shrink back into her chair. Now he was used to her, she didn't look so bad, dressed in a cheerful maroon skirt-suit with her hair freshly curled. Perhaps she'd needed to lose weight. "Excited?" He swallowed another mouthful of tea. "I wonder how much it's changed."

"De-es!" Bev nudged him, and none too gently, though fortunately not on the side that was balancing his teacup.

"What?"

"It's a surprise, remember?" She shot him the how-stupid-can-you-get look she'd been throwing his way since he was six years old.

"Are you sure that's a good idea?"

Bev scowled. "Are you sure you want to spoil it?"

"It'll be delightful, wherever we're going," said their mother. "Will Susan be joining us?"

Bev sniggered. "They're not together anymore, Mum. You know that."

"Oh, I thought maybe…"

Because she'd come to the funeral. Des unfastened the top button of his shirt and loosened his tie. He generally went around in jeans on his days off, but Bev had suggested the suit. But he needn't have listened; sure, the hotel was upmarket but the dress code couldn't be that strict.

"Anyway," said their mother, "we'll have a lovely time just the three of us."

Bev didn't quibble when he changed into jeans for the drive to the hotel. It made him feel foolish for following her instructions in the first place. All it took to be treated like a grown-up was to behave like one. His sister wasn't an ogre.

She'd been a gem when their father died. While Des was still reeling from his divorce, Bev had not only arranged the funeral, but she'd organised this trip to give mother something to distract her on their father's birthday. Of course, Bev had been closer to their parents, equally at ease with each of them. Women generally more clued in to the emotional agenda, but Bev had seemed especially adept. Certainly he'd never heard her moan about her mother the way Susan and her friends did. He resolved to find a moment over the weekend to let his sister know how much he appreciated how she held the family together.

When he realised the case he'd brought was too small to accommodate his suit, his mother fussed about, looking for an old suit-bag of his father's. Bev said it was lucky they'd booked a late lunch, but soon they were ready to leave. Belted into the back of Bev's car, Des refused to allow himself to feel belittled.

The journey would have been quicker by motorway, but Bev had wanted to recreate an epic childhood journey. Although forty years on the traffic was much denser, it seemed to work. Watching the scenery go by, their mother seemed to perk up. "Are we going to the caravan?"

"My lips are sealed," said Bev.

"Mine too," said Des.

Soon they were reminiscing about the year it rained the entire week and the year they all got sunburned. "We didn't know any better back then," laughed their mother and Des felt that indeed those summers had been glorious, and there was something amiss in him, something petulant and childish, to have kept his family at a distance.

They began to sing simple folk songs, the words coming back to Des with a surprising fluency. "Old Macdonald had a farm." "She'll be coming round the mountain." "Ten green bottles." And then almost as suddenly as they'd started, they stopped, each perhaps in their own way missing his father. Des felt a tightening in his chest with the love he'd never voiced.

As the road snaked through the fells, inducing in Des a slight sensation of nausea, he couldn't prevent his thoughts turning to the failure of his marriage. Susan had asked him to ease up on work to give them more time together, but he hadn't listened. He knew what his problem was, had known for years, but that didn't mean he could do anything about it. Work had been his retreat from the messy business of relationships.

He heard his mother snore. Bev half turned from the wheel to smile. "It would be about here she'd start with her stories."

They'd been as much a part of the holiday ritual as that first ice cream. Their mother's childhood had been one big adventure, far more exciting than any of the stories they could read in a book. But the one about her wartime evacuation had been extra special, because the big house where her aunt had been in service marked the halfway point between home and the holiday resort by the sea.

"I always thought there was something fishy about it." Bev met his gaze in the rear-view mirror.

It was painful to admit it, but he'd never enjoyed his mother's stories as much as he'd made out. Never as much as Bev seemed to. Their mother had been so brave, not shedding a tear when she was whisked away from home with only her old teddy and a gas mask. Much braver than Des had ever felt — and he was a boy. "Fishy?"

"How it was all so perfect," said Bev, as their mother continued to snore.

As the car slowed, Des angled his neck to peer through the front window at the sign of the rampant squirrel up ahead. They used to compete to be the first to spot it; Bev usually won.

Their mother stirred at the tick of the indicator, then resettled herself as the car turned onto the drive. Des didn't know when the country house had been transformed into a hotel, didn't know how many birthdays and wedding anniversaries had passed since it was opened to the public. But he knew his mother had never spoken of visiting in all those years. "I don't know what you mean," he said, the words sounding sharper to his ears than he'd heard them in his head.

They progressed down a driveway bordered with poplars. Tyres crunching gravel snapped their mother out of her doze. Bev pulled up outside the porticoed entrance. Across the tended lawn, the lake shimmered. "You know where you are?"

Their mother's breath was laboured, her eyes wide, her face white. "Oh, my!"

Bev hopped out and opened the front passenger door. "Once we get checked in, you can take us on a tour."

The old woman stayed put. She had told them how, as a child, she'd had the run of the place, hanging out with gardeners and stable boys. Freedom, of a kind, but for whom? Her aunt would have been too busy in the kitchen to supervise.

"Let's leave it," said Des. "There's a fairly decent café at the garden centre a couple of miles down the road."

Bev took her mother's wrinkled hand. "I booked us in here."

Their mother pulled back into the bucket seat, shaking her head. So brave Des had thought her, but perhaps he'd underestimated to what extent. It seemed, for all their closeness, that Bev had too. "Look, she doesn't want to. You meant well, Bev. Now get back in the car and we'll go elsewhere."

Bev cut across him. "They treated you special here, did they? Let's get inside and you can tell us all about it."

Their mother let out a sob.

"Come on, Mum," said Bev. "You can rattle on about yourself to your heart's content. Exactly as you did when we were kids."

The autumn sun shone on Bev's burgundy hair. Des realised there was nothing natural about his sister at all.

CHAPTER 3

Unfolding Drama by Geoff Le Pard (UK)

———•◆•———

People came to see for themselves when they heard about Lim Wang, the Flying Chinaman. The café wasn't large or especially good. Safe food choices, okay coffee, a decent range of teas. The tables were scratched and the chairs mismatched. The crockery too came from several different homes and the décor… Let's just say it was vintage and pass on.

You wouldn't class Lim as a waiter. Not really. He was more a performance artist. He moved at a speed that made watchers feel dizzy. Often onlookers were convinced something was wrong with their eyesight, so blurry was he, as he ran and jumped, twisted and spun. He never spilt a drink, never dropped a plate, always had the right order, the tables cleared and wiped before the customers stood, the bills ready before they asked and the change on the saucer (with a complimentary fortune cookie) before their wallets were back in their pockets.

Rumours started circulating that being served by Lim was a lucky totem. It became common for brides and women wanting to get pregnant to visit. Lim knew, somehow. He would pause, meet their gaze with an unnerving intensity of his own, bow and bestow on them a kiss, as soft as a zephyr on a still day, as warm as a new fawn, as chaste as a novitiate's smile.

In contrast, Lim had no time for the gawpers and rubberneckers who came to spectate. Those who stood at the side and clicked their cameras or hid behind their smart phones. For them, he reserved his best trickery. None of their kind ever captured his picture, beyond a red blur, like a smear of blood across their screen. And often they would leave with a sense of foreboding, of something witnessed that shouldn't be seen, of a future that would be uncertain and likely to disappoint.

Occasionally a journalist appeared, wanting Lim's story. He avoided them with an instinctive cunning. Indeed, editors had given up sending anyone when, one breezy day, Jo Hollow found herself outside the café, unsure why she felt the urge to enter. She was new in town, escaping a troubled past and about to start a new job; the café appeared to be a welcome refuge.

The place was manic yet she found herself sat in the centre of chaos, smiling. Some trick of the light, some noise made her look up, half expecting a bird to be flapping in the rafters. Instead, Lim stood by her table. Jo felt the presence of a multitude of eyes on her as he leant in close and kissed her.

As Lim's kiss misted on her lips she heard, as one might when half awake and someone calls out in the street below your bedroom window, a sad voice say: 'She will be strong but take care.' She knew they were Lim's words but what on earth did they mean?

Before she left, a stream of other customers came up and congratulated her, confusing her more. She stopped one, a grey-haired woman in her fifties, who explained about Lim, about his supposed abilities. Jo laughed and returned to her new office where she shared her strange story with her colleagues.

Jo's editor told Jo, with an urgency that surprised her, to write the story. Jo was delighted; a by-line on her first day. Jo's article the next day sparked a deluge of calls and emails and a series of articles. She was an instant sensation. The women who came forward recalled their own stories — telling of the words, of the warnings and advice, of the love and caring that Lim shared. And of their longed-for pregnancies.

Jo read and reread the emails and bought a pregnancy test. As the stick revealed an unwanted truth something split inside her: on the one hand, despair that the past she thought she had left was now to be her future; on the other, a marrow-deep joy that she would have the daughter she had unknowingly craved.

But if Lim had foreseen all this, why did he tell her to take care?

Only Lim had the answer, of that Jo was sure. Many people had sought to uncover who Lim really was outside of the café: where did he go after work; where did he live; where had he come from; how did he know what these women wanted? Needed? But no one had succeeded in tracking him down. A veritable Pimpernel.

Jo became obsessed. She spent large parts of her day, seated near the exit, watching him perform. He provided her with the drinks she didn't know she craved until he put them in front of her, morsels of food that she ate with a certainty she needed them. In that café Jo felt fulfilled; outside she felt nauseous, fragile, and febrile. Inside she was safe — time moved in smooth slow sweeps; outside she was on edge and the hours fractured into jagged minutes, jabbing with deadlines and deceits.

Stories, scribbled in an unfamiliar hand in her notebook, came to her in that café. Wild, strong, compelling tales of refugees and escape. Slowly one story began to dominate. It took shape without her being conscious of why she wrote it.

A young man, of modest circumstances, found himself responsible for his family after his father left to fight a distant unnamed foe. In hunting for food he saw the daughter of the town's leader and fell in love. But she was spoken for, too good for the likes of him. Despite the futility of his love he could not stop its growth.

The young man confided in one person, his oldest friend. The friend's advice: take care.

But the young man was reckless; he decided he had to talk to the daughter and, one day, as she took her afternoon walk he manoeuvred himself to the other side of the fence which gave her shade.

The young woman was bored with her constrained life and frightened of her betrothed. When she heard the voice she stopped; she listened and, for want of better, she flirted. If the motivations at the start were different soon the two people developed a fondness, an understanding, a love.

The war, meanwhile, came closer. More men went to fight. Fear seeped into the town and people talked of escape. The young couple heard the stories and decided they had to escape, to join the flows of humanity seeking a better life in the north, where others headed. The young man and his best friend planned and plotted the lovers' escape. His mother and sister were sent ahead with smugglers, monies provided by the young woman from her dowry fund.

The day came when the couple were to go. Tension was palpable. The enemy was close, a day or two away. But the girl's father heard of the rumours about his daughter. He had her followed and realised the truth. So he sent for the young woman's loathed fiancé; the wedding must take place immediately.

Somehow she sent a note to her lover. His friend delivered it. 'Be at the station at 2', it said. 'She has a car', said his friend.

Anxiously the young man waited in hiding until the appointed hour and headed for the station. But the young woman was not there. Only her distraught maid remained, her face wet with tears.

'Where is she? I came as she asked.'

'But you are too late, sir. She is to be married and has been taken away.'

'But...' He took out the letter. 'See. I am here. At 2.'

The maid placed the letter on the floor and smoothed it. Hidden in the crease an unseen '1' sat next to the '2'. The young man sank to his knees. 'What shall I do? What shall I do?'

Jo stared at the story, a fog filling her head. She had no ending but it couldn't end there. As Jo looked around she realised the café had closed and she was alone. Lim, everyone had gone.

Sadness enveloped Jo. She felt for the couple. She needed to know their fate. As she pulled her coat about her shoulders to deflect the rain and wind she struggled to imagine how the story might go. So in her own world was she that she failed to see the figure in the doorway, tightly wrapped in a grubby sleeping bag and packed around with cardboard to keep out the cold.

She would have gone on, walking further and further into a depression from which she felt no end — where that path might have led, no one knows. Instead, a gust of wind, like a hand on her chest, stopped her and forced her to look up. As she stared at the homeless figure a voice filled her head. 'Jo. Jo...'

The sleeping bag rolled back revealing Lim, a smiling Lim. Jo approached, unsure if she was dreaming. He seemed real but surely he couldn't be homeless. Could he?

She knelt next to him, took his hand in hers and asked, 'How does it end, Lim? What did the young man do?'

And Lim smiled and said, 'He ran, like the wind and the rain and the sun and the stars. He didn't stop running until he found his love.'

'And where did he find her, his love?'

And Lim smiled and unzipped the bag and Jo slipped inside next to him. Lim put his hand on Jo's rounding stomach, a soft, touchless touch. 'Here,' he said. 'Will you take care of her?'

And Jo nodded. 'With your help.'

CHAPTER 4

Crimson Sunset by Ann Edall-Robson (CA)

—•◆•—

"You will go to college!"

His Dad had been adamant that he get an education after high school and Scott had fought the idea from the get-go. He couldn't see the need for more smarts when he was going to take over the ranch from his Dad. He had lived there all his life. All he needed to know surrounded him.

"Take business classes." His Dad had insisted. "They will do you the most good around here. You already know how to ranch, now you need to know how to handle the business side of this place."

Again, Scott had argued with his Dad. He wasn't interested in crunching numbers. He had his own idea of the kind of courses he thought would be a better fit with the ranch. He was unhappy when he thought about being away from the ranch because it was his comfort zone. He thought if he could take classes he liked, being away from the ranch for four years of college might not be as bad.

Scott made an appointment with the guidance councilor at school. If he could persuade her to his way of thinking, maybe his Dad would come around.

When he left her office, he was certain his Dad had got to her first. It looked like his future was going to be in business. She told him there were courses in business designed for the agricultural community. She suggested he look into those.

Scott remembered the arguments with his Dad. The man he admired and looked up to for guidance had won. He swore to his Dad that he would be back at Christmas break and home for the summer. For the first three years he was able to keep his promise.

He was anxious about finishing his last year of school. Several of his classes required he spend time out of the classroom, and Scott disliked the practicum part of his schooling. Everything they were trying to teach him, he had known for as long as he could remember.

He argued constantly with the instructors regarding ranch know-how. Most of them had never set foot on a ranch, let alone got horse manure on their boots. There were a few who had taken him aside and told him to keep quiet about his knowledge. One had offered to give him an A+ and pass the course if he didn't show up again.

During his final semester, Scott experienced two events that would change his life.

The invitation to meet with the Board of Directors of the college had not come as a surprise to Scott. The rumour mill was rampant with conjecture regarding letters sent to the Dean's office about his conduct in the practicum classes. His future with the school did not look good. What concerned him most was that he had not been summoned to the Dean's office first.

Scott arrived at the appointed time and was ushered into the board room. He was expecting some form of word configuration that came from the President's mouth.

"Young man, you have proven to be a thorn in the side of some of our teaching staff. It is obvious that your background knowledge lets you to think you can usurp their authority."

Scott didn't like what he was hearing. He opened his mouth to argue his point of view but the man raised his hand.

"You'll get your chance."

Scott had a pit in his stomach. Whatever was coming next from this man at the front of the room, Scott was certain would be disastrous.

"As I said, your actions are not appreciated. But you do have an exceptional ability to convey the curriculum to your classmates. And you do it in a way that allows them to understand what is being taught."

Scott felt the change in the tone of the meeting.

"Where the hell is this going?" he mumbled.

"This meeting is not to reprimand you or dismiss you from the school. Although both are warranted. It's to give you something to think about over the next few months."

From the back of the room, a young lady moved forward towards Scott. She handed him an envelope and returned to her seat where she had been taking the notes of the meeting.

The President lifted a sheet of paper and started to read.

Scott couldn't believe what he was hearing.

The man ended by saying, "What we are offering you is unheard of. A teaching position with the college, at your age, unprecedented. The formal offer is in the envelope. We will meet again in two weeks to answer any questions you might have. We would appreciate your decision before the end of the semester."

With that, the other members of the board rose and they all left the room. The young lady at the back of the room came over to Scott.

"Congratulations," she said, holding out her hand in an offer to shake his. "That is some coup d'état you pulled off."

Scott was in shock. The thoughts racing through his mind made him oblivious of the woman standing before him.

"Hello! Earth to man who just got a job at the college," she said with a laugh.

He realized someone was speaking to him and focused on where the sound was coming from. "Sorry," he said acknowledging the young woman. "Can you believe that? They want me to teach and I'm not even finished with my degree."

"You are one lucky fellow. People go for years wishing for what you were offered."

The two young people left the board room together. Stopping at her desk when they reached the reception area, Loren watched Scott continue towards the stairs. She smiled to herself and thought, he's in shock.

"What do you mean you're going to turn it down?" came a voice of reason from the other end of the telephone line. "This is the best thing that could have happened to you."

"No, Dad, I need to come home. My job is there. It's what we agreed on four years ago."

"Well, I don't think it is. You can carry on doing what you've been doing since you left for college. Come home at Christmas and be here to help during the summer when school's out. When the time's right, you can come home to stay."

There was a decisiveness in his Dad's voice that said the subject was now closed.

Scott's teaching position started in the fall. The actual job with the college started immediately. His first task — rewrite class outlines. Bring the course curriculum up to a modern and realistic way to teach about ranching and agriculture.

He had added his own codicils to the contract that the Board had agreed upon. It would be a five-year contract with the option to review each year. Leaving the contract early would not affect his severance or benefits. He had negotiated for extra time during reading week to help with calving. His classes would not start until the middle of September to allow him to help with shipping cattle in the fall. At any time should his Dad need him to be full time at the ranch, he was gone.

The next years of Scott's life were full. His teaching methods were a hit and his classes had wait lists.

An introduction to the young lady he had met the day he received his job offer resulted in a courtship. The second summer after they met, Scott and Loren were married.

His Dad had been right.

Scott spent the summer at the ranch and his wife would join him at the start of haying season. Loren had learned to drive the tractor and make bread. Both had earned the city girl brownie points from her father-in-law.

The summer they got married, he had shown Loren the spot where he wanted to build their home. They had stood on the hill, making plans and watching the sun go down. Scott told her that her hair reminded him of the crimson and gold sunset they were watching. She had laughed at him. Calling him an old-fashioned, hopeless romantic.

It had taken three years for the two men to finish building the log house. It was Scott and Loren's home when they were at the ranch during the summer months. With the completion of his contract, it would soon become their permanent residence.

Loren had known, before they married, the ranch would be their home. She had feelings of trepidation over her role as a full-time ranch wife. At first she had been reluctant about the move. At times seeming almost remorseful and unhappy.

The young couple made the decision to sell their house near the college. They accepted an offer from one of the faculty. They had discussed the logistics of the situation. Seeing to the legalities and finalizing the sale had fallen on Loren's shoulders. She would stay with friends until the sale was complete.

It was stormy the day the paperwork finalized. Loren decided she would leave for the ranch and her new home. She wanted to surprise Scott, she said. Their friends had tried to convince her to leave in the morning after the storm had blown over.

"Don't worry. I could drive that road with my eyes closed," she quipped.

Crimson reds, smatterings of yellow, fading into the blackening sky. Standing in the open door of the log house, he watched the sun set over the foothills.

It had not been many years since he'd brought her here as his wife. Hoping she would love the rolling hills and the house he had built for her. She never said it, but he knew she was unhappy.

He would stay on. This had always been his home and in his heart it would always be hers, too.

As he turned to go in, he heard her voice call his name.

He spun around to nothing but the sound of the evening breeze. The gentle wind that reminded him of his wife's fingers trailing across his cheeks.

He sucked in his breath. The sunset and breeze were heartless. Teasing and taunting him with memories until the blackness of the night took over, flaunting the reality that Loren would not be coming home. Ever.

CHAPTER 5

The Journal by Georgia Bell (CA)

It wasn't that I didn't love my grandmother. I just didn't know her very well. But you're supposed to feel sad when someone in your family dies. You feel sad and cry. It's accepted. My friends had all hugged me awkwardly that morning when I told them she was dead.

"I'm sorry she passed," Kate said and looked away.

I nodded and tried hard not to roll my eyes. I never understood why people couldn't just say it. "Passed away" was such a euphemism. Why did the actual words freak everyone out so much? We all knew what we were talking about. Death. Ceasing to live. To breathe. To be aware. She wasn't passing somewhere else. She was in a coffin. Waiting for us to gather around her, stare, cry, and then get on with our lives.

"What hymns shall we sing at her service?" my mother had asked this morning, her smile brittle. I stared hard at the table and continued eating my cereal, refusing to look at her.

"Oh, I know! Let's sing the one about the angels at the gates of heaven," Surrey said. She smiled her bright, bullshit smile at my father. "Gigi would have loved that, right, Dad?"

He nodded once then pushed his chair back from the table. "I'm sure she would have," he said, walking out. We were all quiet as we heard him go downstairs into his office and shut the door.

"I'm sorry," Surrey said. "I didn't mean to make him sad."

"It's okay, sweetie," my mom said, rising and brushing crumbs from her pleated skirt and somehow patting my sister's back at the same time. "It will just take some time."

My sister shrugged and kicked her feet against the legs of her chair, attempting to hum the melody she had suggested. My mother had made us go to church every Sunday since I was a baby, but my Dad didn't attend. Gigi had never come with us, either.

I suppressed the scowl that hung just behind my eyes as I looked at my sister. Suck up. Six years younger and forever trying to be the baby they all pretended she still was.

"That's not how it goes," I said, getting up and grabbing my bag. "And Gigi didn't give a shit about angels."

"Georgia!" my mother called. "Enough."

"Georgia, you coming?" Kate called.

I jerked my head away from the inside of my locker and followed her and the others to class. It wasn't as if I had even really gotten along with Gigi that well. My father's mother had lived everywhere but here. Her husband had died just after her only child, my Dad, had left for university. Everyone had expected her to find another man, someone to take care of her. She was from that generation, after all. She hadn't. She'd sold just about everything she owned and moved to Thailand.

Seriously. Thailand. She was 42. Next, Vietnam. Then, inexplicably, Houston. Then to Indonesia and Nepal. And then, finally, back to Canada. But by that time she was struggling with names. She'd had a hard time remembering who I was and kept calling me by my mother's name. She'd always sent presents though. Postcards. Carved wooden boxes that smelled spicy and warm. Herbs in small packets that she said were for strength, or vitality, or enhancing your aura. I wasn't sure what an aura was.

Her visits had been brief. A week here when I was five. Ten days when my father and I flew to London and stayed with her brother while she was visiting, too. My mother had stayed home with my sister on that trip, who was too little to travel and too precious to be foisted on someone else. My grandmother had seemed exotic and frightening and exciting on that holiday. I didn't know her. But secretly, I had always wanted to be like her.

"Georgia, what about you? What are your thoughts on euthanasia?" My ethics teacher gave me one of those tightlipped "ha-ha, I caught you daydreaming" smiles.

I smiled back and shrugged. "I would rather die a meaningful death than live a meaningless life."

Her smile changed from smug to perplexed. "Who said that?"

"Corazon Aquino," I said. "The first female president of the Philippines."

"I see," she said vaguely. "Good, well, then." She moved on to another student.

Kate chortled from behind me. "Nicely done, Rain Man."

"Damn straight," I said under my breath. I had a memory for quotes. I couldn't hold numbers in my head to save myself, but words stayed with me. Haunted me even, sometimes.

Walking through the front door after school, I groaned and rubbed my shoulder where my school bag, heavy with books, had left an indent. I let it drop to the ground and swore as my laptop tumbled out onto the hallway linoleum.

"Fuck's sake," I said.

"Georgia." My father's voice was muted.

"Sorry, Dad," I said quickly. I wasn't used to him being home.

"Come here."

I felt my heart beat faster. I didn't know what to say to him today.

"Sorry, Dad," I repeated, sticking my head in through the office door.

He was sitting cross-legged on the floor. It was so unusual that I backed up a step. My big, gangly Dad, who said little, but laughed a lot, was sitting in the middle of a pile of boxes, his eyes red rimmed.

"Take this," he said, and handed me a thick, leather-bound book.

"What is it?" I asked, stepping forward quickly and then moving back to the doorway again.

"I don't know," he said and looked at me. There was so much sadness in his eyes. "But she wanted you to have it." He waved a piece of paper at me as if this explained everything.

"Okay. Thanks." I turned to leave. "Dad?"

"Uh-huh?" He didn't look up.

"I'm sorry about Gigi."

"I know," he said. "Me too."

I ran up to my bedroom.

The book was leather bound, gilt edging on each page. It looked like the copies of the bible I'd seen in the hotels we'd stayed at, heavy with must. My mother would check the drawers to make sure there was one there before we knew we could stay. She said it made her feel safe. My father just sighed.

I opened the binding randomly. I wasn't sure why my heart was pounding. It was just a journal. My grandmother's big loopy scrawl spread across the pages. Different colours of pen. Sometimes pencil. I flipped another page and smiled, scratched my fingernail across the writing. Sometimes even crayon, it seemed. I flipped again. Started reading.

The sun is hot today. Hotter than I thought a sun could ever be. It feels like an oven and I have become a small roasted bird, frying in the pan inside. Not that I mind so much right now. The prickling of my skin helps me remember why I came here. Who I came here for. Who I left behind.

It was only the ache in my back that made me stop. I squinted at my dim bedroom, the setting sun leaving me in shadow. My leg had fallen asleep, tucked under me as I had sat on my bed. I shifted and gasped as the blood rushed back in, pins and needles making me laugh and whimper. I reached up to click on my bedside lamp and turned to the front page where my grandmother had written her name.

Georgia Gillian McIntosh.

My namesake.

I traced each letter. Imagining my finger was her pen. That her life would somehow be closer to mine if I could only understand what she had been thinking that day she'd left everyone she loved. I started again. This time at the beginning.

I've been sick for weeks. They told me it would happen, but I didn't believe it could be this bad. Today is the first day I've felt well enough to sit up and write. It seems unreal that I'm even here, never mind being taken care of by an elder in some remote village in southern Thailand. He comes in to my hut every day, clucking his tongue at me and chanting. I was frightened at first, but my fever had taken all my strength and he had just laughed when I tried to bat him away. Now, stronger, he waves his hand around my head and smiles encouragingly as I try to stand up, or hold my own cup of water. He held me once, when I cried. I had been thinking of Jack, all the way across the world, studying so hard. Trying to be a man so quickly now that his father is gone. Those without children will never know the love you can feel for the small people you create. Sometimes I think them lucky.

"Georgia? Honey, it's after midnight. Are you still awake?"

Reluctantly I put her journal down. Padded to the door. My mother stood with her arms crossed.

"It's late and you haven't come down at all tonight." She glanced at the journal on my bed. "Are you okay?"

"I'm fine," I said. "Dad gave me Gigi's journal."

"Yes," she said. "He told me." Mouth twisted. "I wish he'd spoken to me first. I just don't know what she's written in there."

"Nothing out of the ordinary," I said. "Although there is a recipe for freebasing heroin."

"Georgia, that's not funny. You are just being funny, right?"

"Good night, Mom," I said. "I'm kidding. I'm fine." I shut the door.

And opened my other world back up.

I slept very little that night. But my sleep, when it came, was full of rich dreams and vibrant colours. I felt as if I had touched a life that wasn't my own. Lived through someone else's eyes. When I read the last page, I had sobbed. Finally sorry for the loss of this woman who I had never known.

I rose with the dawn and went down to my father's office, where he once again sat sorting the boxes from his mother's life.

"Dad?" I said quietly. He looked up. "Thank you so much. Can I say something tomorrow?"

He looked puzzled.

"At Gigi's funeral. Can I speak?"

He nodded. "I hoped you would."

✳✳✳

I stood in front of them all. My hands shaking. My breath shallow. I could feel the skin on my cheeks growing hot, spreading fire down my neck. Towards my ears. I didn't care. I had something to say. I had a story that I had to tell. Words that marked her life far more than her death.

I cleared my throat. "She started and ended the same way. Fragile, dependent, full of curiosity and wonder. In between her first and last breath, she learned to love, to hate, to be brave, to forgive. She learned that grief made her life more meaningful and taking risks is what kept her alive. She became stronger than she thought she'd ever be, and softer too. Able to soothe the glorious, savage beast her body brought into the world. She watched the tiny boy grow into a man she loved as much as the one she had lost. She had lived. She was proud."

PART 4: ESSAYS FROM MEMOIRISTS are not typical to flash fiction anthologies, but the Rough Writers are not an ordinary literary community. Each of these memoirists is a flash fiction Rough Writer, and each has shared this non-fiction genre with fiction writers in the community. Each essayist examines the experience of writing flash fiction, noting differences and similarities. Each essay expands the idea of flash fiction serving as a writing tool beyond a fiction form.

CHAPTER 1

From Memoir to Flash Fiction and Back
Again by Sherri Matthews (UK)

A funny thing happened to me on the way to writing my memoir. I discovered a writing genre known as flash fiction. Two years hence, the symbiotic relationship between the two forms continues to enhance my writing in ways I never would have imagined.

By late 2012, the twists and turns of life handed me the unexpected opportunity to pursue a writing career, my life-long ambition. But although I had always written in some form or another — be it angst-filled poetry and song lyrics as a teen or journals on and off throughout my adult life — I had no idea if I could *properly* write at all. As for the thought of ever being published, this was as remote to me as the possibility of having tea with the Queen of England.

I didn't know where to begin with writing the memoir that had burned inside me for over thirty years (and anyway, aren't only famous people allowed to write their memoirs, I wondered?). I had no connections in the publishing world and as for even daring to call myself a writer? No way. It was writing creative non-fiction assignments for a home correspondence course that gradually gave me the confidence to submit a few articles to magazines, which, to my amazement, got published. Greatly encouraged, I at last settled down to writing my memoir, starting my blog at the same time.

Creative writing and memoir is where I naturally *sit*, where I feel I have always belonged. It calls to me with a strong conviction that this is what I need to write. I *feel* the flow, I *own* the story, compelled not only in the writing of it, but also in the sharing of it with others when it is complete. My brief and feeble attempts at writing fiction never gave me this. In fact, I had developed a mental block, believing that it wasn't for me. Admittedly I was young — twelve — when I wrote my first short story, but the memory of it sticks with me today.

It was supposed to be a mystery, my first effort at making up a story. I called it 'The Telephone', but my family laughed when I read it out to them. I took the joke and laughed along (it was pretty funny, I admit), but I got the message my stories weren't any good and I gave up writing fiction. But my writing dream never died.

Not until decades later and feeling a little braver, I submitted a short story which won runner-up for a magazine competition. No one could have been more shocked or delighted as I. But still struggling with fiction phobia, I got around the *fiction* thing by basing it on a true story from my childhood. Thrilled with my win, nevertheless, I considered it a one-off, the idea of writing a story with made-up characters, plots, and twists remaining to me an anathema.

Disaster struck when I next attempted to write a short story for the fiction part of my course, producing a piece that was stilted and uninspiring. When I admitted my struggles to my tutor, he suggested that perhaps I wasn't cut out to be a writer after all. Ouch. After that, the thought of writing fiction turned my blood to ice, and I turned all my efforts back my memoir, vowing never to attempt another short story. And then, one year later, I met Charli Mills through blogging, and my writing world turned upside down.

Curious after reading a 99-word flash fiction on my friend and fellow memoirist Irene Water's blog, I clicked on the link to Charli's blog, Carrot Ranch, and the rest, as they say, is history. Terrified to take part at first, I revealed my trepidations to Charli, but her kindness, understanding, and gentle encouragement gradually restored my battered confidence, convincing me to join in. With a wonderful group ready and waiting to cheer me and one another on at The Congress of Rough Writers, I felt immediately accepted and welcomed. Naturally, I went for it.

Flash fiction is a wonderful exercise in tight writing. My early attempts pushed 300-plus words, leaving me wondering how on earth I was going to convey the same story in only 99 words. But with practice in the art of cutting (and I can understand Stephen King's famous quote 'Kill your darlings' so much better now), my earlier waffle vastly improved. Gradually, this process became more natural and transferred over to my memoir writing; one paragraph became a sentence, dialogue turned short and sweet, scenes pruned with less flowery description.

Writing memoir is intense, and I need to come up for air. Having the *distraction* of writing flash fiction each week helps deflect from the memoir focus and gives me a fresh approach. It energises me. Writing in the third person brings relief from the concentration of writing in the first-person POV of memoir. There, I have to recreate the young woman I used to be with no room for expansion or embellishment; I need to craft scenes and bring the inner struggle of the person whose story I am telling (me, then) while reflecting as the narrator (me, today).

When I turn to flash, I can let rip. My characters can say and do what they want and not worry about truth. I am often surprised at the darker elements of my flash stories, but I realise that is because I am probably working out some of the issues from my memoir in my made-up characters. For instance, if there is rage, jealousy, or pain, I can write it out in ways I would not be able to do so in my memoir, because I have free rein.

At other times, the flash takes a humorous turn, and sometimes my characters return for a mini-series. Can this really be happening to me, a memoir writer? This has been the biggest surprise of all. Could these blocks of 99-word flashes, when put together, make up the outline of a more complete story? Horror of horrors, I think. This can't be happening, can it? After all, I can't write fiction, remember.

Memoir is truth, bringing the reader into the writer's authentic experience. Fiction takes us into worlds that the reader knows aren't real, allowing their imaginations to fly, but it still needs to be plausible. With memoir, the reader knows the story (no matter how 'far-fetched' it might appear at times) is plausible because it actually happened. Therein lies the challenge to reveal the truth while also being careful. Many times I've written a flash that would seem to have nothing to do with my memoir, yet so often it reveals a dark and complicated aspect of my true story in new light, rejuvenating parts with lightbulb moments as I find a description or a piece of dialogue or a reflective thought that I might otherwise have overlooked.

Essentially, the 99-word limit has helped me overcome the 'fiction freeze' barrier that plagued me for so long by teaching me to write fearlessly. It's as if someone has sprinkled fairy dust over my creativity, freeing me to write and let go. Before I started writing flash fiction, I could never understand how fiction writers seemingly pluck characters and storylines and plot twists out of thin air and produce stories and novels the way they do. The very thought still stops me in my tracks, but writing flash alongside memoir has opened up possibilities for my writing that I didn't think existed.

Whether writing about a Californian sunset or the English countryside, the laughter of children playing on a beach or the pain of divorce, I have at last come to understand that I can turn even one tiny seed from the stories of life that unfold before me every day into a 99-word flash fiction filled with scenes and characters of my own.

Ultimately, writing flash fiction gives me permission to explore anything and everything, and it lets me soar. When I return to my memoir, delving into the past and bringing truth into the light, I remember this and I am not constrained by the obvious limits set by memoir. I soar there too. And maybe, just maybe, I'll write a novel one day. But not yet. For now, I'll happily stay with memoir and flash fiction, and that's just the way I like it.

CHAPTER 2

In Praise of Nine-Year-Olds with Vision by Paula Moyer (US)

———◆•◆•◆———

There's a folder in my cabinet in my office. It's labeled "Forbidden Engagement" and contains a one-page, single-spaced, typed story by that name. The paper is brittle with age; the typing, in blue ink, bears the marks of a 1950s manual typewriter. It's my first story, and it's perfectly awful — way too much happens on that one page. But you'll have to give me a break: I wrote it when I was nine years old. I had been copying a story out of one of my mother's magazines, those "women's magazines" like *McCall's* and *Ladies' Home Journal*. When I showed my mother my work, she completely dismissed it and said, "Anyone can copy. Why don't you write one of your own?"

So I did. The plot was very similar to what occurred in women's fiction of that time, except that it all happened in about 200 words. But that original effort got my mother's attention. Both of my parents were impressed enough that my father typed the story. My mother kept it for me until I was in my late thirties, when she passed it on to me.

Sarah Brentyn and Charli Mills asked me to write an essay addressing the role of flash fiction in my life as a memoirist. As I have thought about the question, though, I have to broaden the scope: How does flash fiction fit in with my whole life as a writer? Quite frankly, the weekly flash prompt and the subsequent publication mean a lot to my identity as a writer. Like so many writers, I felt the call early in life. However, in this life as we know it, most of us cannot support ourselves on our creative work. One's day job may be writing, but in those cases, often one works as a technical writer or reporter, as I did for over 20 years. The writing in those cases is completely separate from the work that calls to us from our bones and says "write me," and the paid work competes for our time and energy with the creative work. When a writer's day job does not entail writing, often it's the humble work of slogging away at Starbucks, bar-tending, or selling sheets and towels, as I do now in this post-recession world. Therefore, I need the regular recognition, the "likes" on my submissions, the community's generous comments and praise.

As a memoirist, many of my flashes are really memoirs. They are usually from my own life. The "Jean" character in my flashes is me; Jean is my middle name. Recently, my sons have shown up in the flashes, but they have morphed into daughters. "Lydia" and "Nola" are the names that their dad and I had picked out if they had been girls.

Regarding the connection between flash and memoir, my first, reflexive answer was complete bafflement. "There's no connection at all," I wanted to write. "End of essay." That response is, obviously, not true, in some ways. If we were talking about my body, the question may easily have been, "How do your sleep habits help your dietary choices?" At first I would be baffled, and then I would see that, since both sleep and eating are happening to the same body, they are inextricably connected. In the same way, writing in one genre helps me write in another, even if the connection isn't immediately obvious to me.

Yet, let's not leave the "no connection" response as just dismissive. I derive a clear benefit from the parallel-universe way memoir and flash fiction come from me, and this is how: I feel completely free when I write flash fiction, precisely because I don't define myself as a fiction writer. With only 99 words and the weekly prompt, the flash quiets down the "Inner Critic." Every writer knows and dreads it. The niggling voice inside me says something along these lines:

Your memoir is really just therapy. It will have no value. No one will believe that a retail employee has actually written a memoir.

However, since I don't think of myself as a fiction writer, I don't worry about whether my flashes are good. When I write them, I really have no idea whether they're good or not. On the rare mornings when I wonder about their quality, I say, "It's only 99 words. What could go wrong?" And then I keep writing.

Occasionally the flash has been a precursor to a memoir chapter or "chapterlet." "Keep Calm, Stay Alive" is an example. This flash was based on a true story from my father's life as bank examiner. By some fluke, the bank he and his team were examining was robbed while they were in the bank, and my father was standing at a teller's window at that moment. He quickly thought of a lie to get the robber to leave without exposing the fact that my father did not know how to open the drawer. In the flash, I imagined the thoughts my father had as the gunman went from one teller's window to another. I have since expanded those 99 words into a 1,200-word scene for my second book. Often, though, the flashes end up in a folder on my computer, never to be seen again.

Does that mean that my efforts have been fruitless? Far from it. The weekly flash helps build my writing practice and, as I mentioned earlier, gives me regular recognition as a writer. Right now, the first draft of my memoir, *An Inheritance of Spirit*, is complete. The next task is revisions. Coughing up something new every week re-energizes my writerly self and, I hope, will give me a sharper eye for the 60,000-word manuscript that is drumming its fingers on my desk.

Speaking of my manuscript, I would be remiss if I did not mention the benefit of The Congress of Rough Writers in my writer's life. Last winter another flash fiction contributor, Geoff Le Pard, asked me to serve as a "beta reader" for a novel of his. "Beta readers" peruse and comment on a book before publication, and writers typically do this for each other as a courtesy. Later in the fall, when I completed my first draft, Geoff returned the favor and gave generous, helpful comments. We were able to do this for each other precisely because of the community that Charli has created with the weekly flash fiction prompt. We would not have met otherwise: He is in England, and I am in the US, in Minnesota. He writes fiction and I write memoir. Finally, he's a guy, and my book has a definite late 20th-century woman's outlook. He helped me find the blind spots and shorthand that bore the marks of place and gender. As a novelist, his questions showed a laser-sharp sense of timing, story arc, and character development.

The assignment before me was to articulate how flash fiction helps my work as a memoirist. The first answer is "the two are unrelated," or more precisely, "because the two are unrelated, the help is invaluable." The second answer is "the two are inextricably related."

To the extent that flash fiction frees me from being my own worst editor, the practice brings me back to that nine-year-old reading the magazines her mother has beside the couch, scrutinizing the stories' structure and saying, "I can do that."

I can do that. I do it every week. And in ways that I don't always understand, the practice feeds all other aspects of my life as a writer and reminds me that, whatever else is going on in my life, I am called to write.

CHAPTER 3

How Flash Fiction Helps My Perfectionism by Lisa Reiter (UK)

———— ·◆·◆· ————

It was 2012, and I was 46. It was day two of a course in cognitive-behavioural coaching when it finally dawned on me that other people, normal people, do not seek perfection in everything they do. Apparently the negatives outweighed any potential positives, most of the time.

It's one of those crystal clear memories. I remember the exact moment: where I was, who I was with. I remember a rush of adrenalin and an audible "oh" escaping my mouth and all those other evidently more perfect people around the table looking at me with a mixture of sympathy and superiority. I blushed with shame.

Six months on and despite a growing cloud of self-doubt because I hadn't become the next Tony Robbins overnight, it wasn't the perfectionism that caused me to abandon coaching in favour of writing a memoir, but the rapid loss of significant friends in quick succession to cancer.

I'd had a terminal cancer diagnosis in 2000 and survived it. That survival needed writing about. And Ted, who had just died, had told me so.

It wasn't a difficult decision, but it has proved to be a difficult undertaking. Whilst rewarding in many ways, it isn't enjoyable. My memoir is full of dark and difficult triggers for bad dreams, so getting around to writing parts of it has been self-torture. On top of which it had to be perfect.

I set about learning about writing memoir. I joined sites and discussion forums, and I read books, loads of books. I was going to be qualified to write and write well. (Oh dear, still perfecting.)

So perhaps it's a bit of a leap to understand how I ended up writing flash fiction.

I had been blogging for a few months — only because someone told me would-be writers need to. It also seemed a way to keep company online while working in solitude. Wording those first few blog posts was bad enough, so even now I have to pick apart events to understand how I ended up adding fiction to the mix.

Another blogger suggested a particular prompt was right up my street because it was nearly memoir.

Get real! I laughed inwardly. I'd be terrible. I can't make stuff up.

I didn't give it another thought, except for hours spent concocting all the excuses I was going to reply with.

Later, chopping vegetables for dinner, the image of a grumpy old man popped into my head. He was wearing a donkey jacket tied round the middle with baler twine.

I shook my head. No, not for me. Wasting time when I should be writing memoir. I washed broccoli and set it aside and got back to writing for an hour. I was trying to write about a kitchen I'd spent a lot of time in when my imagination brought "Seth" in. Oh no you don't. Get out! You don't belong here. He left muttering.

Later on, clearing away the dinner things, I thought of Seth with a plate of bread and cold cuts. He sat at a small wooden table, chair scraping across a dirty stone-flagged floor, dingy room but a coal fire managing to ease the chill. I was trying to work out whether he'd have a tomato on his plate when he threw a bit of something to his dog and ruffled its head. I heard an affectionate grunt. What's your story then, Seth? I was asking him now, so it was too late. Damn you. I'm not sure I even like you.

Now I was muttering. I grabbed my iPad and poured him out. I let him rest overnight. In the morning I tidied him up a bit and let Charli have him. Just 99 words. I justified it on my blog by being tempted by the novelty and the link to memoir. It wouldn't happen again.

In truth, I'd already had the idea of posting my own memoir prompt, and I could see how community-minded other bloggers were. Many of the Carrot Ranch participants took to all sorts of prompts. Would they road-test mine? It turned out they would, despite some finding it a difficult genre. Charli was straight in there. A lot of her writing is flavoured with the context of her own history, so she's no stranger to memoir even though it's not her thing. It didn't seem reasonable to excuse myself from her flash fiction simply because I found it difficult.

In my head I committed to participating, but several weeks went by. I kept looking at the prompts. Clearly fiction was not my thing. Nothing clever nor interesting popped into my head the way Seth had.

Then came a prompt for a travel horror story. I snuck a peek at the early submissions. Wonderful foggy railway stations and all things I wish I could conjure. Something about the horror aspect kept me worrying at it whilst I went about my day. I broke it down. Travel — about moving from one place to another. Vehicles. Wheels, engines, motors… Suddenly it came to me. I'd recently had a bone scan. A motorised bed inches the patient under the scanner. The faint noise of the motor is the only company you have for the 20 minutes it takes. I put a character through 99 words of something similar, managing not to reveal what she was travelling on or why until the end. I was pleased with what I'd written. Pressed "publish" no problem.

A month went by and again the prompts didn't appeal, and the agony of terrible ideas was eating up disproportionate amounts of time. Perhaps I should focus on memoir after all and not waste days agonising over 99 words of make-believe.

But then a month later I easily made someone choose between her own life or that of her unborn baby for "clashing priorities." It seemed relatively easy to interpret prompts with cancer or death! The challenge for me would be to really make something up.

Finally after another lapse in time, I made up 99 words of something about unicorns. It was cheesy.

"It's okay," my husband said.

"OKAY?!"

I let it rest for another day, tweaked bits, and re-presented it.

"Yeah, it's all right," he said.

"ALL RIGHT!?" (Needs more work, then.)

The deadline loomed. I worried at it all the next day. Simon looked frustrated as I passed over the printed piece when he came in from work.

"Yes. It's fine."

"FINE?!"

"Yeah, it's good enough," he said.

"But you don't like it?"

"Honestly it's fine."

"What do you mean by fine? What's wrong with it?"

"There's nothing wrong with it. It's just not my kind of thing, that's all."

"Ugh. I can't submit it."

"Why not?"

"It's obviously not good enough!"

"Good enough for who? Who's going to care!?"

"People who read my blog."

"You're writing a memoir. This is just a bit of fun."

This was not fun. I felt miserable. He was getting bored.

"Isn't this a bit perfectionist?"

That winded me, because yes. It was exactly that. I had given about three days of my life over to 99 words about unicorns and no one would care whether the final line should have a different adjective. My heart was racing. Were embarrassed friends really going to call to caution me they couldn't be associated with me if I ever did anything like this again?

They'd most likely

A) Read it in a hurry because they're my friends and felt obliged.
B) Be grateful it was a short post.
C) Not read it at all because it wasn't what they were following my blog for.

Anyone else reading it was probably participating in the same prompt and

A) If it was terrible, would be compassionate with an obvious novice.
B) If also novices, would not realise it was terrible.
C) Would not even read it!

I checked what other people had published. Some were not much better, but nobody was unkind in response. The deadline hung over me. Three days' work could go to waste or I could "practice" being less than happy with something. I pressed "publish." Nobody came to the house to take me away or shut down my blog. My friends didn't break contact.

Then I realised I was on to something. And it wasn't the fiction.

That first year it felt like I spent half my life on flash prompts. In reality I published something eight times in 52 weeks. When I hit the sweet spot, it was fab. When I missed, it was agony. I still spent days avoiding it or days overworking something, but I knew I shouldn't let it drop. I tried strategies like looking at the prompt just before the deadline or containing ideas to things I already knew about. Nothing seemed to help at first because I just wasn't good enough.

You can't always distil perfectionism from reasoned self-doubt or attention to detail, but you can spot it in certain behaviours. It's of clinical interest, disordered behaviour, when it stops you doing small things and things you really do want to do that won't harm others. (It can be a good thing in certain situations: think concert violinist, brain surgeon.) My kind of perfectionism means procrastinating writing projects I dearly want to succeed with. Either they grind to a halt or never start. (If I don't start, they can't be bad.) But things like ironing don't get done either because I think I should get around to the writing first. Or the house is dirty because cleaning the bathroom takes up two hours because I obsessed about removing lime scale around taps using an old toothbrush.

The cognitive-behavioural way of fixing these issues, as with most behaviours, is to practice new and better, more helpful, thoughts and actions and congratulate yourself for doing so. Iron five items, not the whole pile; just wipe the taps. The lime scale can wait. Congratulations! There's still time left to write. But it's much harder to see with the actual writing. Having a go at being imperfect means moving past phrases that don't quite work or making do with the first thing that pops into your head rather than waiting hours for the sixth idea in case it's better. Wanting to write a perfect memoir had paralysed the first draft. I was still rewording the first 10,000 words whenever I opened the file. To finish the rest, I realised I needed to practice being content with something "good enough" and moving on to write the next bit.

Inadvertently, practicing flash fiction in a constrained time period forced me to do just this: To be satisfied with 80 percent rather than dwelling on the 20 percent further potential. I learned in a very small way to get over myself. I am good enough. The words are good enough. Move on.

Without expecting to, I realised after a while I was more comfortable putting imperfect words into the memoir. I learned that getting anything down gave me more to work with anyway. I learned the hard way that that is simply part of producing a finished product.

Now I look at a flash fiction prompt before I have to drive or walk somewhere — I use the time to churn a few thoughts.

Later I write down what came to mind. Sometimes I see how I want it to end or begin. Other times I have a scenario in mind. Then I splurge 80 to 120 words into a file. I leave it alone for a while. I make sure I'm busy with something else. Later I'll race myself to try and edit in 15 minutes. Finding a picture to post with it takes longer! (It doesn't actually need a picture — still perfectionist...)

Then I let it go. Like a captured bird, it's better gone. And there's no harm done. There really isn't any harm, even if it is crap. Read that last sentence again if you recognise perfectionism in yourself. Because I'm beginning to feel good enough by practicing the thought and forcing myself to behave that way.

And remember, it isn't really about the writing either. It's about whether I'm going to let worrying about being good enough stop me doing things I want to do. The answer has to be no, and the discipline of a little flash fiction is a good way to practice that.

CHAPTER 4

Flashback: How the Practice of Flash Fiction Hones the Craft of the Memoirist by Jeanne Belisle Lombardo (US)

———◆———

For the writer, flash fiction is a condensation of its parent form, potent liquor distilled out of a more diluted brew. For the reader, it's a shot knocked down in one burning swallow, not a mellow bottle imbibed over a long evening. So how can the practice of this shortest of literary genres help writers of longer forms, in particular the memoirist and her near cousin, the novelist?

To answer that we must first remember that whatever the length of a narrative, certain considerations come into play: where to begin and how to end a piece; how to structure a story and create a narrative arc; how to be authentic; and on a scene level, how to decide which details to include. And so it is with flash fiction. Structure and rigorous selection matter, even (especially) when working in a form defined as a story of fewer than 1000 words — and at Carrot Ranch, a mere 99 words.

So a story is a story is a story. But when it comes to craft, one of the advantages of flash fiction is the writer's ability to produce multiple pieces in a short time, to learn through doing. As Charli Mills explained in a recent post celebrating the 99th Carrot Ranch Flash Fiction Challenge, her original vision was to create a place "where writers could learn to access creativity through problem solving (the constraint); write from a unique perspective (diversity); [and] read and discuss the process or prompt (engagement)." In engaging in this kind of literary experience, writers would also use the challenges "to explore our ideas, characters, longer works, craft and more."

These goals precisely align with the benefits I have observed since discovering and exploring flash fiction at Carrot Ranch. I wandered into the Ranch about a year and a half into a long memoir project for a client. Now, having completed the book while practicing flash fiction, I see three distinct ways working in flash fiction has impacted —and improved — my writing as a memoirist:

- Identifying the essence of the story or scene
- Developing an authentic voice
- Using "prompts" to explore deep memories and connecting memories to themes

"The Art of Omission"

Despite its brevity, the flash form is not a mere exercise in description or characterization. Rather, it may be considered one scene in one chapter in a novel (or memoir) pared down to its essential elements. Flash must have a clear beginning, a middle that moves the story forward and reveals what we need to know about the character(s), and a point to it — an end that brings closure in some form: perhaps a decision on the character's part, an epiphany, a resolution of conflict, or a change in the character. It must have an arc.

To achieve so much with so few words, the writer of flash fiction practices what Grant Faulkner calls, in his article "Flash Dance" (*Writers Digest*, May/June 2015), "the art of omission." Because flash has as its currency "the small but telling moments of life," not the "grand arc of a lavish story line," the writer must dispense not only with unnecessary detail, backstory, and involved transitions, but also with any elements that do not support the core point of the piece: the meaning of that snapshot of a moment in a life. The writer must remember that the action in flash moves "through small pivots, rather than major events."

Though the novelist and memoirist have much more scope within which to move, this focus on the moment and the telling detail is applicable to storytelling of all kinds. This is because what determines a successful story is as much about what the writer leaves out as what she puts in it. As Annie Dillard warns in William Zinsser's anthology *Inventing the Truth: The Art and Craft of Memoir*, "You have to take pains in a memoir not to hang on the reader's arm, like a drunk, and say 'And then I did this and it was so interesting.'" In flash fiction, we absorb that lesson the first time we try our hand at it. Flash fiction simply doesn't give the writer any leeway to veer off into topics not connected to the essential story.

That focus on economy was perhaps the toughest but most illuminating (and liberating) early lesson for me, one that came after scribbling reams of detailed scenes edified with copious research into blocks of dense, boring narrative. I was struggling to break my client's life story into meaningful scenes instead of long passages of pure exposition. Around the same time I came across an article about the connection between scenes in a movie and scenes in a novel, and following this course of inquiry came across a master in the field.

In his acclaimed guide to writing, *Story: Substance, Structure, Style, and the Principles of Screenwriting*, master writer Robert McKee teaches writers that every scene is a story event. In every scene there is a value at stake. Exposition cannot be the sole justification for a scene. And every scene is built of "beats": a change in behavior, and action/reaction. Once I began to practice flash fiction, I connected McKee's insight to the form. It occurred to me that flash fiction is like one of these beats, a glimpse of a character's life that may suggest preceding and following moments and actions but that stands complete in itself.

I still have much to master in this area. Writers do what they do partly because they revel in words and metaphor and other literary devices, and it's a challenge to rein in the creative urge. But when I rewrite a scene now in my client's memoir, I approach it as if it were a flash, or a series of flashes. I look first for the instigating action or moment, the telling detail in the characters' behavior or speech, the pivotal action in the scene, the change or epiphany. Flash has honed my perspective and helped me eliminate the "noise" that distracts from the real power in the scene. In a recent comment on her blog, Charli Mills describes a similar use of flash technique to strengthen scenes in her novel. "I think the revisions are coming along well," she wrote in a comment on her website, "because when I put a scene into flash, I have a better sense of the characters and stories compared to when I started out using the flash to figure out the story and characters!"

Practice Makes Perfect…and Honest

Of course, effectively honing any piece of writing down to its essence is easier said than done.

All writers must remember the shock of first putting pen to paper and expecting the ravishingly eloquent lines that had pumped through their heads to magically transcribe themselves onto the virgin page. Then the hard reality that writing is not simply inspiration but craft. And that craft requires regular practice…work! It's the old 10,000-hour rule, the adage that genius is 1 percent inspiration and 99 percent perspiration. So we stretch our fingers, turn off our email, and face the screen…every day.

But what do we write? Some days the work-in-progress (WIP) doesn't budge. The new story idea entices, but vaguely, from an unbridgeable distance. That's when the practice of flash fiction is invaluable. Not only do we write, we write to a prompt and within a strict word limit.

This seemed an easy enough charge when I first began to turn out my short short stories. But just as when I had first tried my hand at memoir, I was confronted by the same basic decisions about selection, structure, and meaning. That is where practice comes in. Writer Dan Blank from WEGrowMedia stated the obvious recently in a daily post on creativity from the Writers Unblocked blog: "The more stories I tell, the better I get at it." And while this is true of any writing, because flash fiction, with its word and time limits, does not give writers the luxury of long, slow edits, the result can be a less polished but more honest and authentic story. While the writer may want a more sculptured narrative in a finished work, it is through the very limits and demands of the form that flash fiction hones the singular voice we each have. And sometimes the form may even support the achievement of Hemingway's well-known maxim: "All you have to do is write one true sentence. Write the truest sentence that you know." Simply put, a regular flash fiction practice encourages greater honesty in one's work. And honesty is what puts the best memoirs leagues ahead of lesser efforts.

The Prompt: Direct Line to Memory

Finally, there's the prompt, which much of flash fiction begins with. The prompt is a long-used aid for writers, one that stimulates creative thought and exploration of themes. When working in memoir, the prompt also serves as a direct line to memories.

It's my guess that novelists are nearly as prone as memoirists to pilfer their memories for nuggets: details about a character; particular smells, sounds, sights and textures of a setting; a dramatic episode. But in memoir, the writer has the double duty of crafting an effective story and being true to the memory. This latter task can be frightening. The writer feels exposed, unsure about revealing intimate details. Yet, whether the writer presents the story as flash fiction or "flash memoir" (what writer Lisa Reiter calls the "Bite Size Memoir"), it is the honest plumbing of the memory and the connection of the memory to a theme that can create a powerful piece.

With a full-length memoir, the writer may not use prompts as such for each scene. But the practice of using prompts in flash fiction prepares the memoirist for the task at the heart of writing meaningful scenes in memoir. This is because, unlike autobiography — the straight telling of a life from beginning to end with as much historical accuracy as possible — memoir recounts a selected portion of a life told through the prism of a theme or lesson or guiding idea. With memoir, one narrows the frame at the outset, and this defines the selection of scenes. What a striking similarity to the spirit of flash fiction! Indeed, acclaimed writer and teacher William Zinsser could be teaching us about flash fiction when he tells us in *Writing about Your Life* that we must "Think small. Don't look for 'important' events but rather the small, self-contained incidents that are still vivid in memory." What you remember about the past, Zinsser reminds us, is, after all, where the larger truth lies. Because flash fiction is all about those small, self-contained incidents, they are then also, like memoir, where a larger truth lies.

End Notes

Mostly I have talked about craft here, but I will end with one last observation on how flash fiction impacts the writing of memoir. That's how the community that forms the core of Carrot Ranch and other groups serves not only to bring writers together in a common endeavor, but in so doing also supports the three points highlighted here. Through reading other writers' flash fiction pieces, I've gained a sense of what works: how a wide variety of writers achieve their unique and authentic voices; how the astute selection of small details creates intriguing characters and settings; how writers connect to their pasts and use memory to enrich their writing. But more than that, such a community has allowed me to develop my skills as a memoirist in a safe place, one where I know my flash memoirs — no matter what the topic — will be received openly and with an understanding of the common goal that unites all of us: the development of our craft. That is everything…because that sense of safety has allowed me to trust my own instincts. And self-trust is what allows us to grow in our art.

CHAPTER 5

Defining Differences Between Memoir and Fiction by Irene Waters (AU)

———— •·◆·• ————

Each week, on Thursday, I sit at my desk in front of my computer reading the flash fiction prompt put out by Carrot Ranch's lead buckaroo, Charli Mills, hoping I will be able to put fingers to keyboard with ease. Sometimes I can dash out my 99 words with fluidity; at other times I wonder if I'll make the week's deadline for submission. Writing fiction is not what I am accustomed to as a memoir writer, and yet each week I look forward to the challenge. Sometimes I ask myself why?

I have enjoyed writing ever since I can remember. I was probably directed towards memoir at an early age as my second-grade school teacher squashed out any creativity I may have had when she admonished me for writing about a puppy found in the mud when the given assignment was to write about mud. My Dad kept my writing alive when he gave me a diary that same year and showed me how I was to write in it, making a record of the facts of the day and my reflections on how I felt at the time as a consequence.

I write creative non-fiction, that is, a true story told well, and in order to do this I employ fiction writing techniques, such as dialogue and high definition scenes, to make the narrative vibrant and compelling. When I came across the 99-word flash fiction prompt I decided to give it a go, thinking that it would not be that difficult. I knew that, eventually, if I was to continue writing, I would either have to turn to fiction or start writing about writing as, having written my life, this would be the only life I had left to impart. I believed few fiction writers make up their characters or their stories from scratch, but rather, use real-life people and situations to create their unique characters. I thought I would continue to 'write what I knew', a mantra of many of the writing workshops I have attended. Amos Oz, a French author/memoirist, in responding to a question about what was auto-biography and fiction in his narratives, said, 'Everything is autobiography: if one day I were to write a love story between Mother Teresa and Abba Eban, it would no doubt be autobiographical, but it wouldn't be a confession. All my work is autobiographical, but I've never confessed'. The reality of writing fiction proved to be a little more difficult than I expected.

Initially I used history or articles in newspapers to give me my inspiration. It was not long before memoir also was where the bones of the story came from and rarely, but occasionally, I managed a flash that was pure fantasy. When using memoir as my base I always fictionalized at least one element of it. It may have been where the event happened, an ending which differed from reality, or the addition of a character, and I was elated when I managed to get that unexpected twist at the end.

One of the big differences between memoir and fiction is the characters found within the text. In fiction these characters are made up by the author whereas in memoir you have a responsibility to the person whose autobiography you are writing in the process of writing your memoir to portray them honestly and without rancour. Writing fiction gave me a freedom I had not experienced before as I told stories I would never write as memoir, that is, I fictionalized snippets of my own life or those of people I knew. At times, however, I wished that I had taken ownership of the identity I portrayed, for I believe that is the purpose of memoir, the creation of an identity.

Identity formation fascinates me. I believe that memoir is essential in its creation. We all tell our memoirs every day in the recounting of incidences in our lives, and at other times such as writing our curriculum vitae, personal advertisement on the dating site, and even our obituary. All these form an identity. When our memory fades and we lose our ability to recount our memoir, our identity fades, along with the memories we can no longer bring to the surface. Paul John Eakin suggests that memoir is a homeostatic function which keeps us anchored to time and place, allowing us to know where we are when we waken and how much time has elapsed between going to sleep and reawakening. It is the telling of these memoirs and showing the relationship between the 'I' character that is being narrated and the other people in the narrative that shows not only the 'what' of the 'I' character who is being narrated but also 'who' they are. However, our identities change depending on whom we are with, over time, and where we are placed in the cultural and social world and so too do our memoirs. I believe that writing memoir is not done to remember the past, but rather to create a future. Writing flash fiction gave me insights into these differences as I discovered a major problem I had when writing flash fiction.

The first difficulty I encountered was naming the characters. At first I believed this was because all the names I thought of were names attached to people I knew, and it made writing difficult as the character then seemed to take on the characteristics of the person who already owned that name. Then I realized it was a little more involved. Naming people in memoir poses no difficulty, as the characters come with their name attached, but in fiction, the choice of name can add significance to the character and give it layers that are impossible to obtain when writing memoir. These names can be ones which have a strong association with a known character, such as names from the bible, mythology, and history, or they can be invented. Charles Dickens was perhaps the most prolific inventor of names, with the names forming characteristics he wished them to portray, such as Ebenezer Scrooge and Oliver Twist. At first the problem of naming stymied me and I didn't name my characters at all. This resulted in a flash that seemed colourless. Over time naming both people and places became a challenge and part of the fun of flash fiction. I used names like Perspemon, Tristam, Bergdis, and Allard, which gave added meaning to the flash.

Another difference I have discovered between fiction and memoir lies in the understanding by the author of scenes outside the normal every day, such as writing criminal activities, stories of unicorns, and historical events, and being able to convey these characters in a way that convinces the readers that this 'is' how a real-life person would act. Of course, the secret to writing these fiction pieces has to be a combination of research and good powers of observation. In memoir, research is not required or, if carried out, it is on a limited basis, as in the writing of memoir one is relating one's own life from memory. Indeed, this is perhaps why some people write memoir and others write fiction. Fiction could be defined as portraying an understanding of the world outside the author whereas memoir is an understanding of the world within; for the reader they are therefore consumed for two very different purposes. For me observing comes as second nature. I would not have made the grade as an intensive care nurse if my skills of observation were poor. My husband is subjected to many fabrications as I regale him with intricately woven tales of unknown people we see in the coffee shop or pass on the street, so although I haven't, before venturing into flash fiction, written the genre I have enjoyed observing, then creating. I also enjoy researching, and this foray into fiction has satisfied both these aspects of my personality.

The 'flash' side of the challenge was also beneficial to my writing memoir. In 99 words there is no room for unnecessary words, and each word had to perform a function in the work to deliver a complete, compelling story with beginning, middle, and conclusion, with the necessary amount of tension building and character development. This made me acutely aware of my own writing. Active voice, the preferred mode for both fiction and memoir, uses fewer words and creates more immediacy than passive voice. Dialogue and scene description could also be practiced in the flash, leading to an increase in vibrancy for the memoir I was writing.

As a memoir writer, therefore, participating in flash fiction prompts had some major benefits. Writing flash fiction became a tool under which questions of genre and purpose for writing memoir became exposed. It made me examine closely what the differences were of the two genres, which often mirror each other in form. Despite finding that it challenged me, at times to my limits, it also allowed me a freedom of expression that was impossible to achieve with memoir as the memoirist is compelled to convey the truth. I found I enjoyed the challenge and although I am foremost a memoir writer, it is now not outside the realm of possibility that I may try my hand at fiction when I have exhausted my life writing. Finally, writing flash has honed my technical skills more than I anticipated, and the practice gained from the weekly event has been translated to my memoir, helping it become a more finely tuned, vibrant narrative.

PART 5: BUILDING COMMUNITY WITH FLASH FICTION by Norah Colvin (AU)

This anthology begins with a collection of 99-word *(no more, no less)* flash fiction stories compiled from pieces written by a diverse group of people from around the world who gather weekly to respond to a prompt at Carrot Ranch, an online literary community.

The group is fluid rather than formal, with writers participating when interests and schedules allow. While regular participants quickly begin to feel comfortable with each other and with the process, bonding in a literary community, occasional participants are always welcome.

Participation means different things to different writers. For some, it's the sheer joy of writing; for others, it's an exercise in improving writing skills and techniques or maybe for trying out ideas for works in progress. Some simply thrive on the challenge. Many writers integrate their responses into posts inspired by the prompt; others contribute standalone pieces. Some share their first drafts; other pieces are polished.

Belonging to a literary community or group for discussions about reading or writing, or to critique literature -- a body of written works -- has many benefits; for example, individuals may be empowered by the development of critical reading skills and the challenge to take creative writing risks.

Many literary communities are closed, with restricted numbers of participants exclusive to a demographic, such as school, club, or workshop. Others require participants to meet certain criteria, such as writing ability or goals.

Open and inclusive writing communities that welcome readers and writers with differing experiences and interests can be formed online or in person at public libraries or open mic events. Focusing on the shared enjoyment of reading, writing, and discussion, more than on publication or graduation, these communities help make the literary arts accessible to the general population.

Flash fiction can be used as a cornerstone for the development of such literary communities.

Though a small literary act, with its length and time constraints, flash fiction can have big results. When strangers come together, be it in a library, classroom, coffee shop, or online, to share writing and ideas, bonds are formed and a community can develop. Whether intent on practicing craft or on expressing creativity, a supportive community helps to develop confidence and pushes writers to take risks in finding creative solutions.

The unique response of each writer challenges others to consider different approaches and perspectives. When compiled, the combined voices communicate a more inclusive and diverse view of the topic, possibly ranging from something as simple as "a fish" through to more complex ideas such as "an expression of compassion." It is through the appreciation of the group's diversity that connections are made.

A simple formula for building a community using flash fiction is to introduce the constraint (including word length and response time), offer a prompt to stimulate ideas, and provide opportunities for participants to share their responses and to give and receive feedback.

Flash fiction has something for everyone, whether reader or writer. If you enjoy reading flash fiction, you may also find it rewarding to write. Why not give it a try?

What is flash fiction?

Flash fiction is a form of short writing. In its various forms, it may be known as, for example, micro fiction, sudden fiction, or six-word stories; the length may vary from as few as six to as many as 1,000 words. Brevity is a constraint, and writers attempt to pack as much story as they can into few words. Each word must count. There is no room for "darlings," let alone a need for them to be killed.

What can be done with 99 words? Anything at all. A revolution can happen. A world can change. A couple can fall in love. A heart can break. Ninety-nine words can lend hope to those in need.

It's a moment or a lifetime. A quick touch of contact in passing. It's inspired. It's the last rays of sunset held in a hawk's outstretched wings. A cloud of breath on a frigid night. It can be a new dawn, a realization, a gasp of salt water mist. But most of all, it's a story. It lives through words.

Choose wisely.

Pete Fanning, Virginia, USA
Rough Writer
99 words

As previously noted, the flash fiction pieces included in Part 1 of this anthology were written in response to weekly prompts. The intent of the prompt was to spark, rather than restrict ideas. Although constrained by the 99 (exactly) words and the requirement to respond in less than a week, writers had the freedom to interpret the prompt as they wished.

Organizing with flash fiction

If setting up a flash fiction activity for a group or class, the following suggestions may serve as starting guidelines:

- Issue a prompt. This may be an idea, a phrase, or one or more specific words.
- Set word count and timeline constraints. These can be adjusted to suit the needs of the group and may be influenced by whether the writing is done in the group or away from the group.
- Provide opportunities for participants to share individual responses.
- Engage participants through positive feedback. Respond with encouragement and support targeted to individual needs and writing goals.
- Publish responses in a compilation.

When using this model in a group setting, encourage participants to take turns leading the activity. Build in opportunities for reflection on the way in which the flash fiction writing evolves over time, and discuss breakthroughs writers may experience as they become more comfortable with the form, process, and group.

Reading and writing flash fiction reawaken my students' love of storytelling. One-word topics and photo prompts for flash fiction are innovative precursors to longer writing opportunities.

For my lesser-skilled writers, a four-minute writing task is a nonthreatening daily experience. After finding a personal topic worth exploring, they beg for more.

When it comes to skill-building, flash packs a punch. Using authentic, literary silhouettes, my students identify figurative language devices, recognize an author's style with word choice and sentence structure, and explore the world of inference.

Facilitating a flash lesson is a far more worthy investigative experience than a worksheet.

Roger Shipp, Virginia, USA
Rough Writer
99 words

Further uses of flash fiction

In addition to being an effective tool for improving writing skills, flash fiction is attractive because it requires less of a time commitment than larger works. Consider how flash fiction can be used to:

- **Develop**: Play with traits one flash fiction at a time to develop a character before drafting a fuller story.

- **Revise**: If a large scene lacks focus, write the scene as a flash fiction to get to the heart of it.

- **Experiment**: Test different twists and reactions to solve plot difficulties experienced with longer works.

- **Practice**: Learn poetic form by writing its story as a flash fiction.

- **Refresh**: Take a break from an intense project, thesis, novel revision, or work by writing creatively to a constraint.

- **Write tightly**: Edit to the exact words needed to learn the power of brevity and clarity.

If you struggle to control the flow of words, to tell and not show, then flash might be the answer. The discipline of a word count can seem daunting. You have an idea but you've barely set the scene when the limit is breached. Worry not; you're not alone. The beauty of using a prompt is you get to see how others do it; how they pare back to the fundamentals, how they leave so much unsaid yet the reader knows what they mean. In essence, flash makes you trust the reader. Once you've acknowledged that trust, you'll fly.

Geoff Le Pard, London, England
Rough Writer
99 words

How to use this anthology

The prompts from Part 1 may be freely used for ideas by book clubs, as ice-breakers for workshops, or as practice exercises in writing groups or in the classroom. If involved in outreach to marginalized groups, such as developing healing activities for women's shelters, teen programs, or prisons, consider how flash fiction can be used to encourage personal reflection and self-expression. Though brief, the rewards for those who practice can be mighty.

> Of course the prompt helps to steer a piece of flash fiction, which can be biographical or complete nonsense. Having to narrow the amount of words helps as a natural editor, creating a concise focus. Well if one wanted to pretend to be concise...

> So now what is the value of writing flash fiction? It's a discipline in an otherwise hectic, chaotic and creative world of an author. A place for memories, humor, and creativity. A "flash in the pan" of letters used as ingredients to sentence a tasty serious stew or a silly succotash. Rib stickers each one!

JulesPaige, USA
Rough Writer
99 words

Qualities of a writing-based community

Qualities differ from rules. Qualities are the — often unwritten — under-standings that drive the ethos of a group and may vary between groups. When joining an existing group, it is important to observe ways members respond and interact. If forming a new writing community, you have an opportunity to guide its culture. These are some qualities to consider:

- **Be welcoming:** Regular, occasional, and new participants are more inclined to join in if they feel welcome.

- **Encourage playfulness:** The opportunity to think about ideas playfully, in new and creative ways, gives even serious writers inspiration and new writers confidence to try their ideas in a supportive environment.

- **Be inclusive:** Welcome writers from a diversity of backgrounds, abilities, interests, and goals to enrich conversations and make connections.

- **Inspire:** Encourage writers to respond in ways that demonstrate their unique ideas and skills.

- **Encourage exploration:** Try new topics and genres; read works of others and interrogate their techniques; find new ways of expressing ideas.

- **Provide safe opportunities for sharing:** Respect writers' unique ideas and perspectives; use them as windows to new understandings.

- **Give writers a purpose:** The opportunity to share, receive feedback, and publication (even if only within the group) provides an incentive for writing.

- **Provide positive feedback that supports a writer's development:** The secret is in providing feedback targeted to an individual's need. Some may require simply an acknowledgement, such as "I enjoyed your story." Others who are working towards publication may desire a more detailed analysis.

- **Be supportive:** Be mindful that the purpose of a writing community is to *encourage* writing. All activities and interactions should provide opportunities for writers to develop and share their skills.

How to encourage and support writers

When using flash fiction to build community, it's important to remember that participants benefit from a supportive environment. When discussing ideas, there is no right or wrong to individual perceptions or interpretation. Always respect the writer.

Giving feedback takes practice. Go softly. Be positive and encouraging. If you want deeper feedback or someone asks it of you, continue to abide by the qualities that make a community a safe place for such critique. For example, ask for clarity if an idea is hazy or ambiguous. Instead of offering a negative opinion on word use, look for, and comment on, what works.

Use words you would like to hear. Start and finish with a positive statement; be encouraging and constructive in the middle. Unless you are doing the final edit before publication, there is no need for harshness.

These are some community-friendly tips to keep in mind when responding to the writing of others:

1. Read as a reader. What do you like? What appeals to you?

   Be positive, be polite, be encouraging.

2. Ask questions to gather information and gain greater understanding. Instead of making suggestions or giving criticism, simply ask what you need to know more about, such as what weren't you sure of or what confused you. Explain your understanding and see if it aligns with the writer's intent.

   Be positive, be polite, be encouraging.

3. Make suggestions that encourage the writer to think in new ways, not to impose your own ideas, such as "Have you thought of...?" "What if...?" and "How could...?"

   Be positive, be polite, be encouraging.

4. Respond to the writer's needs. There may no need to go into further detail unless the writer asks for help to revise, edit, or proofread. Not all pieces need be publication ready.

   Be positive, be polite, be encouraging.

Do flash fiction communities require rules?

Rules are important to flash fiction writing communities. They provide transparency and ensure that everyone in the group knows how to participate.

Below is an example of rules used at the online Carrot Ranch community which may explain how a group operates and what the parameters of the activity are:

1. Follow the weekly blog post for each new flash fiction challenge.

2. Respond with 99 words. Exactly. No more. No less.

3. Include the challenge prompt of the week in your response.

4. Title is not required or included in the 99 word count.

5. Go where the prompt leads (it's about creative problem-solving not accuracy).

6. Post your response on your blog before the deadline and share your link in the comments section of the challenge you are responding to.

7. If you don't have a blog, or you don't want to post your flash fiction response on your blog, you may post your response in the comments of the current challenge post.

8. Keep it business-rated if you do post it at Carrot Ranch, meaning don't post anything you wouldn't want your boss to read.

9. Create community among writers: Read and comment as your time permits, keeping it fun-spirited.

10. Your response will be shared with readers and published in a weekly compilation.

You can make your own rules to match a group's requirements and may include content parameters, such as the use of profanity or adult content. Rules can be written to target a group's focus or to accommodate a sponsor's requirements. Rules are a way of setting expectations and encouraging others to participate.

No group is too large or too small for sharing stories in a flash fiction community. Take out your pens. Get ready to write!

PART 6: ACKNOWLEDGMENTS AND BIOS

Charli Mills, Series Editor, Keweenaw Peninsula, USA

From riding horses to writing stories, Charli Mills is a born buckaroo wrangling words. She once won a trophy for goat-tying and later, one for storytelling.

With more than two decades in freelancing, publications, sales, marketing, editing, and public speaking, Charli's byline has appeared in *Montana Outdoors, Colours Literary Magazine, Edible Twin Cities,* and online at *USA Today, Livestrong,* and the *Houston Chronicle.* She's published more than 200 print articles, managed an award-winning cooperative newsletter for 15 years, and has been included in *How to Go to College on a Shoe String.*

Charli writes stories set in the American West, giving voice to the experiences of women and others marginalized in history. She searches old newspapers, scrapbooks, and cemeteries for forgotten historical stories.

CarrotRanch.com

Sarah Brentyn, Editor, USA

Sarah Brentyn wrote her first story when she was nine years old and never looked back.

Her work has appeared both in print and online in lit mags, newsletters, websites, newspapers, and anthologies.

She has a master's degree in writing and has taught at both the secondary and collegiate levels. She created and led writing workshops for various age groups from kindergarten to teens.

When she's not writing, you can find her strolling through cemeteries or searching for fairies.

She is the author of *Hinting at Shadows*, a collection of short fiction.

sarahbrentyn.com

Acknowledgments

The Rough Writers & Friends keep the literary community thriving and diverse by writing, reading, and chatting at Carrot Ranch.

Each writer in this anthology has books, blogs, and projects that we wish them much success with. We're thrilled to feature them in this anthology. Thanks for lending your voices.

Thank you to those who helped shape this book, including the extra time and energy individual Rough Writers gave, lending their skills and support: Sherri Matthews, Geoff Le Pard, Norah Colvin, Ann Edall-Robson, Irene Waters, Jeanne Belisle Lombardo, JulesPaige, and our talented Carrot Ranch designer, Ann Rauvola. A special thank you to C. Jai Ferry who is a Rough Writer with two hats: One for writing grit lit and another for line-editing with consistency despite multiple variations of English among our group.

Much gratitude goes out to our dedicated readers: Renee Gerry, Breanne Burke, Marianne Warren, and Joy Cornett.

The Congress of Rough Writers

Anthony Amore, Rhode Island, USA

Anthony Amore is a professor of writing and literature who is also writer and co-creator of a site called The Plagued Parent, where his poetry, fiction, and non-fiction can be found. His essay writing has appeared on The Good Man Project as well as in guest posts for various other sites. He makes his home in southern Rhode Island, along with his wife and teenaged daughter.

theplaguedparent.com

Georgia Bell, Toronto, Ontario, Canada

Georgia Bell is a writer from Toronto, Ontario, who loves reading, coffee, scotch, and chocolate (although not necessarily in that order). She is the author of *Unbound (All Good Things #1)*.

georgiabellbooks.blogspot.ca

Sacha Black, England, UK

Sacha Black is a writer and author from Hertfordshire, England, who blogs, swears, and rants professionally. Wait, no, that's her hobby. She is publishing two books in 2017: *Keepers*, the first in her YA fantasy series, and a writing craft book titled *13 Steps to Evil*.

sachablack.co.uk

Norah Colvin, Brisbane, Qld, AU

Norah is a teacher/writer from Queensland, Australia, who is passionate about education. She has contributed to numerous educational publications and currently shares teaching suggestions and resources online. She enjoys writing flash fiction for the opportunity to hone her writing skills and participate in a community of fellow writers.

norahcolvin.com

Pete Fanning, Virginia, USA

Pete Fanning lives in Virginia and spends most of his time chasing his dogs and his four-year-old son around. He's written more than one novel and has used them to start more than one fire.

lunchbreakfiction.wordpress.com

C. Jai Ferry, Midwest, USA

C. Jai Ferry is an author from the Great Plains in the US who prefers brutally honest characters in need of some form of professional help. Her favorite type of writing is short stories that initially appear innocuous...

cjaiferry.com

Rebecca Glaessner, Melbourne, Vic, AU

Rebecca Glaessner is a writer from Melbourne, Australia, who is a stay-at-home parent of three preschoolers. Her favourite type of writing is science fiction with a touch of psychological exploration.

rebeccaglaessner.com

Anne Goodwin, England, UK

Anne Goodwin is a writer from England who, in her previous incarnation as a clinical psychologist, used to help others tell the neglected stories to themselves and now writes her own. She is the author of two novels: *Sugar and Snails* and *Underneath*, both published by Inspired Quill.

annegoodwin.weebly.com

Luccia Gray, Spain

Luccia Gray is a writer and blogger who was born in London a long time ago and lives in Spain because she loves the sunshine. She writes thrilling novels with unforgettable characters, including *The Eyre Hall Trilogy*.

lucciagray.com

Urszula Humienik, Poland

Urszula Humienik is a writer and editor from Chicago, Illinois (currently living in Poland), who likes doing Sudoku and cooking delicious vegan food for her family and friends. Her favorite type of writing is fantasy.

urszulahumienik.com

Ruchira Khanna, California, USA

Ruchira Khanna is an author from California, USA, who draws inspiration from society. She is the author of two novels and one children's book.

ruchirakhanna.com

Larry LaForge, Clemson, South Carolina, USA

Larry LaForge is a retired college professor from Clemson, South Carolina, USA, who enjoys writing short stories about college, sports, and life in general. He is the author of "Swimming for Pride" and five other published short stories as well as a collection, *The 100 Word Dash*.

facebook.com/LarryLaForgeStories

Geoff Le Pard, Dulwich South London, UK

Geoff Le Pard is a writer/author/blogger/poet from London in England who now writes full time. He has published four novels, with a fifth due in 2018; he has also published an anthology of short stories (with a second also due in 2017).

geofflepard.com

Jeanne Belisle Lombardo, Phoenix, Arizona, USA

Jeanne Belisle Lombardo is a writer, ghostwriter, and editor from Phoenix, Arizona. An avowed plant-whisperer, she is the credited writer on the medical memoir *Backbone: The Life and Game-Changing Career of a Spinal Neurosurgeon* by Volker K. H. Sonntag, MD (Lisa Hagen Books, 2017).

jeannelombardo.com

Sherri Matthews, Somerset, UK

Sherri Matthews is a memoir writer from England who enjoys walking and photography. Her writing has appeared in magazines, anthologies, and online.

sherrimatthewsblog.com

Allison Mills, Houghton, Michigan, USA

Allison Mills is a science writer from Michigan who dances (a lot). She writes for Michigan Technological University and loves geoscience stories.

mtu.edu/news/writers/mills/

Paula Moyer, Lauderdale, Minnesota, USA

Paula Moyer is a memoirist who lives in Lauderdale, Minnesota. For her day job, she sells sheets and towels at a department store, and she's training to be a doula. She does needlepoint for fun and to remember the importance of patience, detail, and color. She's been working on her memoir, *The Inheritance of Spirit*, for a few years and hasn't come up for air to publish shorter non-fiction pieces. Because she defines herself as a non-fiction writer, she finds writing flash fiction freeing.

JulesPaige, Pennsylvania, USA

JulesPaige (or just "Jules") hails from the southeastern part of Pennsylvania, USA. Semi-retired Jane of All trades (mostly retail), her writing has appeared in school magazines, local newspapers, chapbooks, E-Zines, and blogs. Primarily a poet since grade school, she also writes flash fiction.

julesgemstonepages.wordpress.com

Amber Prince, North Texas, USA

Amber Prince is a writer from North Texas who loves hiking. Her favorite type of writing is contemporary fiction with multiple perspectives.

fictionandfood.wordpress.com

Lisa Reiter, UK

Lisa Reiter is a writer from the UK who scribbles memoir and stuff about you she'll pretend is fiction one day. Her favourite writing is probably that raw memoir telling naked truths so you can walk in someone else's uncomfortable shoes a while. She's not been keeping up with her blogging but is sure to let us know when she finally publishes her own memoir.

sharingthestoryblog.wordpress.com

Ann Edall-Robson, Airdrie, Alberta, Canada

Ann Edall-Robson is an author and photographer from Airdrie, Alberta, Canada. When she's not writing, she enjoys gardening and quilting. She is the author of *Moon Rising: An Eclectic Collection of Works* and two cookbooks, *From Our Home to Yours: Cookies* and *From Our Home to Yours: Cakes & Squares*. Her writing has appeared in the collaborative arts anthology *Voice and Vision 2016*.

annedallrobson.com

Christina Rose, Oregon, USA

Christina Rose is a writer and blogger from Salem, Oregon, who currently works in human resource consulting doing business and technical writing. Her writing can be found on her blog and has been published in the *Hiram Poetry Review*. Her favorite type of writing is short fiction and poetry, and she is currently working on her first novel.

thewordyrose.com

Roger Shipp, Virginia, USA

Roger Shipp is a middle school teacher (USA) on the cusp of retirement. Encouraging the love of reading and writing has been his passion for more than thirty-five years. His eclectic interests in archaeology, astronomy, gardening, fitness, and improving his culinary skills have been a unique springboard into the blogging world. He is a frequent contributor to many flash fiction communities. His favorite flash pieces are often historically based.

rogershipp.wordpress.com

Kate Spencer, British Columbia, Canada

Kate Spencer is a freelance lifestyle writer. She invites readers to come and dance through the daisies, sit by the fireplace and reflect upon life and simple pleasures. A few years ago she published a commemorative book exclusively for her family filled with short stories from her father's life.

eloquentlykate.com

Sarah Unsicker, St. Louis, Missouri, USA

Sarah Unsicker is a state legislator from St. Louis, Missouri. She writes as a hobby and uses the power of stories to influence public policy.

Irene Waters, Noosaville, Qld, AU

Irene Waters is a writer from Queensland, Australia, whose pastimes include dancing, reading, and playing with her dogs. Her main writing focus is memoir. Her writing has appeared in *Text Journal* and *Idiom23* magazine, and she is the author of two memoirs which she plans to publish in 2017.

irenewaters19.com

Sarrah J. Woods, Charleston, West Virginia, USA

Sarrah J. Woods is a writer from West Virginia, USA. She loves writing in almost every genre but most frequently finds herself penning essays on personal growth. Her blog is "A Bringer of New Things."

abringerofnewthings.wordpress.com

Susan Zutautas, Orillia, Ontario, Canada

Susan Zutautas is an author from Orillia, Ontario, Canada. She has written a novella, *New in Town*, and two children's books: *The Day Mr. Beaver Met a Moose* and *Mr. Beaver Plans a Party*.

everythingsusanandmore.blogspot.com